# MARKED FOR MENACE

SUSAN HAYES

Marked For Menace (Book Four of the Crashed and Claimed series)

First print Publication: Sept 2022

Editor: Amanda Brown

Cover Art: Croco Designs

Published by: Black Scroll Publications Ltd

# ABOUT THE BOOK

She survived impact... But her plans burned up on re-entry.

Spending her inheritance on a luxury cruise was the most reckless thing Hope has ever done, and she's loving every second of it... right up to the explosion.

Now she's stuck on a strange planet filled with countless dangers and just one chance to survive. The problem? He's huge, scarred, and the scariest thing on this planet. He's also the sexiest male she's ever seen. His protection comes at a price, though. Her.

The life she envisioned is gone forever, but she might be on the brink of finding something better... if she can let go of what she wants and embrace what she *needs*.

# 1



Days like this were a struggle. Not because Menace hated being with his clanmates. They were his brothers, his only family. It had always been them versus the universe, and he'd happily lay down his life to save any of them.

His life would be easier if he *did* hate them, or at least was indifferent to them. If he didn't care, he could leave this place and go live somewhere else. It was a big planet. He'd find somewhere quiet and far enough away he'd never be tempted to see his brothers again.

They were his family, but some dark, primal part of him didn't care about that. Every time he spent too long with the others, his dark side would rouse and pace the confines of the mental cell he'd sealed it inside.

One day, it would break free. On that day, he

feared what would happen. Not to him, but to the only family he had—the fa'rel.

The problem was that he didn't hate them, which was why he was with two of his brothers, helping Mayhem extend the roof of his home. Weaving grass and slender branches into the existing roof wasn't physically demanding work, but what it lacked in backbreaking labor it made up for with mind-numbing tedium.

Still, it needed to be done, and it went faster when they worked together. This week, he and Strife were helping Mayhem. Next week, the three of them would be at Strife's home, and the week after that, they'd all be coming to help him prepare his place for the rainy season.

They'd struggled their first year on this planet. In the beginning, they had nothing but the supplies they'd salvaged from the wreckage of their crashed ship. They'd huddled inside the ruined shell as the rain fell day after day. Being in such close quarters had nearly driven him to the breaking point more than once, and he'd spent most of his time outside. Flash floods, carnivorous wildlife, and the constant rain had been better than being stuck inside with his brothers.

Mayhem worked on the roof from above while Menace worked from below. They'd fallen into a comfortable silence that made it easier for him to stay focused on the job and not the proximity of the others.

The longer he could work uninterrupted, the longer he could stay.

So of course, his brother had to do something stupid. Mayhem growled and tugged so hard at the thatching he was working on that part of it pulled loose and showering Menace with bits of vegetation.

"If you fuck that up, you can fix it yourself." He glared up at his clanmate while brushing plant bits and dust out of his beard. A long blade of orange grass hung from one of his horns and he swiped at it absently.

"You grumble more than Strife when it rains. It's fine," Mayhem replied unapologetically.

His dark side wanted to grab his brother by the horns and drag him through the hole in the roof. Instead, he flashed his fangs and made a joke. "No need to be insulting. I don't grumble anywhere near as much as he does."

A moment later they were caught in a shower of freshly cut branches. Strife had obviously heard them.

"Asshole," he hollered loudly enough his brother couldn't fail to hear. Then he sighed and looked around at the mess. "Now we need to stop and clean up before we can start the next section."

"You're grumbling again," Mayhem said.

He swallowed an angry retort and rolled his shoulders to disguise some of his tension. "One more comment from you and I'm going home. You can finish this yourself."

He didn't want to leave until the work was done,

but it wouldn't be the first time. His brothers understood. They all had the same problem, though he'd always been affected more than the others. He hid it as best he could, but they gave him space when he needed it. The need to dominate was part of their design, but the verexi had—by intention or by accident —ramped his up to dangerous levels.

He rarely thought about the scrawnies—their name for the race responsible for creating him and his brothers. Thinking about their captors only made him seethe and wish for a chance at payback. Not that the verexi were stupid enough to come down to the planet where they'd imprisoned his clan. Losing control of their creations was an embarrassment for them. From time to time, the verexi would hire mercenaries to try and exterminate the fa'rel. Each time that happened, the mercenaries died and his clan would add a few more weapons and other tools to their limited supplies. Hunting down the mercs was the best way to keep his dark side satiated.

As if in answer to his thoughts, a sharp series of beeps erupted. He'd never been here the other times, but he knew what that alarm meant. The verexi's hired killers were back.

It was time to go hunting again.

He followed Mayhem to the small shelter that protected some of their most important assets—a cobbled-together mess of components that allowed them an illicit link to the verexi's satellite network. It warned them when anything entered the planet's atmosphere.

"What is it?" he asked Mayhem once the other male had a chance to look at the monitor. Strife joined him at the door and they both waited for confirmation of what was happening.

"We're about to have company."

*Good*. That would take the edge off his anger and give him a few days of relative peace. Long enough to make sure everyone's homes were ready for the coming rainy season.

Mayhem and Strife knew more about computers and constructs than he did, but he'd seen enough to understand. A cluster of small ships fell away from a much larger one that continued on its original heading. The bigger ship would fly over his territory and should land on the far side of a range of hills while the smaller ships were descending rapidly toward fa'rel territory. In fact, one of those vessels should land in the area he'd claimed for himself.

*Even better*. He'd be hunting on familiar ground.

They watched the screen, trying to estimate where the ships would land. The system lost track of them as they neared the surface, but Menace knew where to start looking. Each of them had a ship coming down in their claimed territory. It was an odd strategy, one none of them had seen before. None of them understood what the enemy was up to. Not that it mattered. They were the enemy and they would die.

"When will they stop trying?" Menace asked, slapping his fist into his open palm.

Mayhem turned away from the monitor. "Let them come. This is our home and we'll defend it."

"To the death," Strife added.

"To the death," Menace repeated, meaning every word.

The three of them butted heads, their horns clacking as they touched. They bid each other good hunting and set out.

Menace didn't bother taking the stairs. He vaulted over the railing a split second faster than Strife, both of them bounding from limb to limb, letting gravity do most of the work.

His claws carved new gouges in thick branches as he descended, slowing him enough to let him land on his feet. He was already sprinting toward his territory when the distinct sizzle of a signal gun discharging sounded followed by an ear-piercing screech intended to catch the attention of anyone who'd missed the light show.

He didn't bother slowing to look. He knew what had happened. Mayhem had sent up a bright green flare, letting the others know a hunt was underway. Since only three ships were nearby, the hunt would be short and simple, each of them dealing with the invaders in their territory. The rest of the clan would prepare their defenses and wait. They didn't have communication equipment. When a flare went up, everyone returned home and got ready. If another clanmate arrived with news, they'd react. Otherwise, they would stay near home and prepare.

Menace raced through the forest, using the shortcuts he'd long since memorized to reach his territory as fast as possible. Their territory was set out in a rough circle, and each of them claimed a triangular section with the crash site at the center. Most of the others had built their homes a short run from the middle.

He hadn't. His house was near the distant boundary of the land he'd claimed for himself, and as it happened, it was the opposite edge from where he'd estimated the ship would land. Going home to gear up would waste valuable time, so he chose a different route—one that would take him to the right area and straight to a cache of supplies he'd placed for this kind of scenario. He didn't know if any of the others had done the same thing, but he assumed at least some of them had.

They'd spent too many years stashing food and hiding what few items they'd managed to create or steal from the scrawnies to stop now. They'd want to be prepared for anything. Just like him.

The cache was stored in a cave partway up a hill. It wasn't large, but it was high enough to stay dry even in the rainy season, and he'd fashioned a door heavy enough to keep out any of the local fauna. He stayed there sometimes when he didn't feel like facing the summer storms that drenched the forest and sent lightning dancing through the clouds overhead.

He only took a few minutes to gear up, tying greaves to his lower legs and securing wide bands of leather to his wrists. He fastened a short kilt of boiled leather straps around his waist and adjusted the fit so it didn't rub the fur over his hips. He hated wearing the thing, but it offered too much protection to forgo it. Not that it would do much against blaster fire, but the mercenaries weren't the only dangerous predators on this planet. Teeth and claws were a much more common threat, and he'd likely run more of them than the mercs.

He grinned at that thought. More than once, the local wildlife had reduced the enemy's ranks before the fa'rel joined the hunt. Menace was fine with that. He was happy to share the kill with anyone or anything, so long as they didn't get in his way.

He armed himself with a variety of weapons and then jogged further up the hill to a rocky outcrop that offered a good view of the valley they called home. The boundary of his land was marked by a slow-moving river they called the bend.

Bysshe had tried to argue for something more poetic, but the android's suggestions were all shot down by the fa'rel. It was a river. It had many bends in it. The name was simple and obvious. Bysshe had muttered about their lack of imagination, which seemed odd coming from the only artificial lifeform in their clan. Bysshe was an honorary member of the fa'rel despite the fact he'd been created by humans. He never spoke about how he'd ended up under the control of the scrawnies, and none of them had pressed him about it. The past didn't matter. Their future was uncertain. All that mattered was the moment and the memories of those they'd lost along the way.

As he scanned the river with one of the few sets of functional binoculars they possessed, he couldn't help but think about one of his clanmates. Rage had been the oldest of them, and he'd done what he could to protect them from the worst of the scrawnies' cruelty. He would have loved this planet with its open sky and stretches of forest so vast you could lose yourself for days. Rage had died in an escape attempt not long before the verexi finally gave up on their experiment and pretended to arrange for the surviving fa'rel to live the rest of their lives on an uninhabited planet. They'd even sent down supplies, though the containers were mostly full of useless gear like bathtubs instead of what was promised.

None of them had any idea why their captors had provided them with anything at all. It didn't make sense. The verexi had promised them a new life, but their plan had always been to kill them. Bysshe had figured that out and warned them once they were on the ship that brought them here. The crash landing was the best they could manage once they had taken the ship's AI offline.

Rage had missed his chance at freedom. He'd died trying to find a way for them all to escape. It wasn't fair. Menace smacked his fist into his flat palm. Nothing in their lives had ever been fair, but losing Rage stung the most. One day they would take the fight to the scrawnies. Then, he'd dedicate every kill to the brothers he'd lost, starting with Rage.

When he spotted debris along the edge of the river, his thoughts of revenge shifted from the future to this moment. The enemy appeared to have crashed their ship into the water. A tiny ship. *Hmm.*

He increased the magnification until he could make it out clearly. Not a ship. An escape pod. At least that's what he assumed based on the fact it had inflated some sort of flotation device to keep it from sinking. He'd initially expected a scout ship, but that wasn't the case. This pod was a one-way delivery system, not really a ship at all.

His grin widened until his fangs showed. If the three small ships were all pods, the larger ship must have had serious issues big enough to make it crash. If they could get to the wreck before the mercs could destroy it, there would be plenty of supplies and weapons to scavenge.

*Today was a good day after all.*

He put away the binoculars, checked his weapons were secure, and set off toward the river. It was time to go hunting.

## 2

———

OF ALL THE new experiences she'd had since coming aboard the *Bountiful Harvest*, Hope's favorite thing had nothing to do with visiting new worlds and mingling with a variety of compatible species for a chance at finding an interested mating partner.

In fact, the actual matchmaking part of the cruise had so far been a soul-crushing, confidence crumbling experience. Instead of being swept away by a kind and loving match, she'd discovered that most of the males who signed up for this kind of thing wanted an exotic beauty they could parade around like a pet. There was no romance in the pairings she'd seen. It was all cold and mercenary, with lawyers on hand to negotiate every aspect of the women's new roles and conjugal duties.

*Conjugal duties*. Even thinking the word made her shudder. She'd signed onto this cruise in hopes of finding somewhere and someone to settle down with. She didn't want to be a pet or breeding stock. Not that it mattered. She hadn't received a single offer.

"Please relax. Take three deep breaths and let go of your worries." The flat tones of the massage pod's AI intruded on her thoughts. The massage pod was her new favorite thing, and she'd indulged in a treatment almost every day.

"Sorry," she apologized. She'd been mocked more than once for her habit of speaking to computer programs as if they were real people, but she did it anyway. Growing up the way she had, she'd spent more time interacting with computers than with people. Despite that, her parents had taught her to use good manners, even if she only had computers to practice with most of the time.

Her first chance to interact directly with new people had been at the hospital where she had finally received the lengthy treatment that restored her immune system. The process had been long and often painful, but she'd distracted herself by making plans for all the things she'd finally be able to do. She just hadn't envisioned doing them alone.

The cruise was almost over and the odds of her meeting someone before it ended were about the same as her being hit by a comet in the next five minutes. She'd heard rumors about some of the offers made to women left over at the end of these cruises. Employment contracts that ranged from domestic help to brothel work. Humans weren't signatories to the Galactic Legion's Unified Agreement, which left them with limited rights and protections.

At least they were recognized as sentient lifeforms, but not every race agreed with that assessment. Those races would be the ones waiting at the end of the cruise. They'd make their offers to the dejected and desperate leftovers, offering some semblance of security to women who had nowhere else to go.

Hope had no interest in signing her life away in exchange for food and shelter. She wanted more out of life than to simply survive. That's what the first three and half decades of her life had been. Her parents had worked themselves to death while she had stayed home as much as possible because of her broken immune system.

Talium-6 was the most valuable substance in existence, but it was also one of the most dangerous to mine. Blasting and drilling into the hard rock to reach the stuff turned some of it into an airborne powder. When breathed in by some lifeforms, including humans, it could trigger an autoimmune response that made the victims vulnerable to a host of diseases and conditions, including something commonly referred to as "Miner's Motley."

Not even the treatment she'd finally been able to afford could remove the pale blotches from her skin, and now she understood that those marks had doomed her chances of finding a match.

The males thought she was damaged goods.

They were wrong. She'd left her home to find a new life for herself, one worth living. Her first plan had been this matchmaking cruise, but she could see that had been a mistake. She'd let herself get swept up in dreams of romance and happily ever after. Now the cruise was almost over, and she'd have to move on to Plan B. Which meant choosing a place to live and then finding a job.

"I need to go over my lists again," she said. Lists helped her organize her thoughts and let her visualize her plan. She'd already made a list of potential new homes and jobs she could do. Like all her important lists, they were written by hand with an antique pen on her precious supply of real paper. She'd only been able to do remote work until now, but since her treatment, she could work anywhere she wanted. Anywhere but home, or any other location where they mined Talium-6. The risk of relapse was too great if she was ever exposed again.

Still, she had options. Lots of them. A lifetime's worth of hopes and dreams all written down, ranked in order of feasibility and preference, accompanied by sub-lists of pros, cons, and other factors.

All she had to do was go over the facts and decide which path to take but not until after her massage. Reality could wait a little longer.

Or so she thought.

It turned out that reality wasn't interested in taking

a number. It exploded onto the scene in a cacophony of screaming alarms and an unsettling groan of metal under stress. At least, that's what it sounded like to her.

The pod door opened while at the same time the bed she lay on rose up on one side, tipping her toward the opening.

The system spoke in the same flat, emotionless voice as before. "Emergency protocol has been engaged. Please leave the pod and return to your quarters immediately. Repeat. Emergency protocol has been engaged. Thank you and have a nice day."

"What is happening?" Hope asked as she scrambled to her feet. Her *bare* feet. Shit. She was naked! Emergency or not, she needed clothes before she went anywhere.

"Emergency in progress. Return to your quarters immediately," the computer stated again.

"So you don't know what's happening either," Hope muttered as she shoved her feet into a pair of spa slippers and reached for the fluffy white robe provided to everyone who used the spa. "Hey, computer? I need my clothes, please."

"Emergency in progress. Return to your quarters immediately."

"Give me my clothes!" She had to raise her voice to be heard over the continuous wail of various alarms. The computer didn't respond to her request. Hope tugged on the robe, tied the belt in a hasty knot, and rushed out of her cubicle. She hoped to see a bot coming down the hall with her clothes neatly cleaned and folded for her.

No such luck.

"Okay, looks like I'm facing this crisis in the buff. Awesome." Lights flashed along the floor, guiding her toward the spa's main doors. Out in the corridor, it was pure chaos. Alarms blared so loudly they drowned out whatever the captain was saying over the ship-wide comm system.

Hope clapped her hands over her ears to muffle the worst of the noise and tried to remember what she was supposed to do. Her quarters weren't even on this deck. Was it safe to use the elevator during an emergency or should she find one of the ladders the crew used?

Before she could recall where the nearest ladder was, a set of airtight doors slammed shut down the corridor. *Shit!* That wasn't good. It also cut her off from what she thought was the nearest ladder. She'd have to find another way off this deck.

The flashing lights and constant noise were disorienting and her slippers were living up to their name. Each time she tried to take a normal step, her footwear slipped. She was about to give up and go barefoot when someone caught her by the arm.

"This way," Rissa called to her.

The older woman flashed her a reassuring smile as she pulled Hope along with her. Rissa seemed to know where she was going, and that was enough for her. "What's happening?" Hope asked.

Reality made another dramatic entrance at that moment. The deck bucked beneath her feet, throwing them both off balance. They managed to hang on to each other well enough to keep their feet, though Hope lost a slipper.

"Bad shit. Maybe an attack," Rissa said. She'd clearly tried to sound matter-of-fact, but Hope heard the note of fear in her voice.

"Attack?" Who would attack them? Why?

A new alarm blared, this one so loud it drowned out most of the others. The lights went out, leaving them both in utter darkness for a brief second. Red strobe lights kicked on, pulsing in time to the alarm.

This was one of the ones they'd covered in the safety briefing. It meant—*shit*. It meant they had to abandon ship.

Rissa must have recognized the alarm too because she shouted, "Come on! We need to go. Now!"

Rissa broke into a surprisingly fast sprint for a woman her age, and Hope followed her lead. They ran pell-mell along the corridor until they finally reached an evac station. The pods were all open and Rissa pushed her toward the one nearest her while shouting instructions.

The last thing Hope heard was, "Hang on, be smart, and don't go too far from your pod."

She nodded once and then hurried into the waiting pod. By the time she turned around and got herself seated, Rissa was gone.

"Thank you and good luck," Hope said as the door sealed. Rissa had probably saved her life, and she hadn't even gotten a chance to say thank you. Hopefully she'd get a chance later… if there was a later for any of them.

At first, being inside the pod was relatively comfortable. It was cramped and the seat harness bit into her shoulders if she tried to move too fast, but once it detached from the ship, things calmed down. No more sirens or flashing lights, and the pod didn't shake or make any of the other worrying sounds the *Bountiful Harvest* had.

The onboard computer spoke to her in a soothing tone that might have helped ease her sense of panic. Might have, except it calmly explained that her escape pod would attempt to land on a nearby planet with a survivable environment. She tried to ask it for more information, but all it did was recite instructions about what to do once the pod was on the planet.

What planet? She had no idea. She didn't even know what it meant by "survivable." She didn't even have a window to look out, and the computer clearly wasn't an interactive model.

Rissa's advice came to her again. "Hang on, be smart…"

Hope nodded to herself, wrapped her fingers in the harness, and focused on the calm voice giving her instructions.

She didn't have anything better to do.

"In case of a water landing, this pod will automatically inflate flotation devices..."

The computer didn't lie to her about the process of landing, but it definitely left out a few things. Her escape pod didn't land. It *crashed*. And it didn't fall straight down to the planet. Oh no. It smacked into something that sent the pod tumbling on all three axes. She screamed, which turned out to be a mistake. She got a mouth full of thick goo as the pod's system filled the interior with suspension gel. It would protect her during impact... if she didn't drown in it first.

That was her last thought before the pod slammed into the surface. She must have blacked out for a few minutes. By the time she was aware again, most of the gel had gushed out through the open pod door.

Huh. The door was open. Either the pod had accompanied her to the afterlife, or the landing hadn't killed her after all. Her moment of optimism fizzled as she got herself unstrapped and leaned out the door for a better look at her surroundings.

*Shit. Shit. Shit.*

When the computer had mentioned a water landing, she'd envisioned an ocean, or at least a nice, calm lake. Instead, she was adrift in a massive river. Not ideal. Especially since her skills as a swimmer were best described as "can dog paddle in a shallow pool for short periods."

One shore was measurably closer, but it was still too far away for her to swim to it safely. Same with the scattered boulders she spotted rising up out of the water.

Besides, both Rissa and the onboard computer had told her it was important to stay near the escape pod. It was her only source of food and shelter, not to mention it would already be broadcasting an emergency beacon.

"Okay. Stay with the pod. I can do that. Maybe I can grab a stick or something and try to steer toward the shore." She spoke aloud because it helped her focus and because she needed to see or hear something familiar. The chirps and twitters of unknown lifeforms filled the air. The sky was the wrong shade of blue, and the flora on this planet was mostly orange, with occasional patches of red or yellow. The grass along the riverbanks was a similar color, and when the wind stirred the blades, it almost appeared to be on fire.

The amount of the suspension gel inside the pod had leveled off at ankle depth, leaving her soaked in the stuff with more of it squishing around her toes. She decided her first priority was to clean up and dry off as best she could.

A quick check confirmed that the pod was floating on an inflated ring that extended out about a meter in all directions and formed a relatively stable platform.

Hope abandoned what was left of her dignity and crawled out of the pod on her hands and knees. It wasn't easy to do while wearing the sodden and not-so-fluffy bathrobe, but she kept it on for the moment.

She made it outside and kept crawling to the side of the float. The water swirled around her strange little raft, but it was hard to see much past the reflective glare of the sun.

She scooped a handful of water up and used it to wash the gel from her face. The goop dissolved away easily, tempting her to keep going. She stretched out on her stomach and plunged both hands into the river up to her elbows, rinsing as much of the stuff off her skin and the sleeves of her robe as she could.

When nothing reacted to her hands, she decided it would be safe enough to dip her feet into the water to clean them off, too. She wouldn't dangle them over the edge for very long in case something decided she looked edible.

The cool water was an improvement over the goopy gel, and it made her aware of how warm it was. Wherever she was, it had to be a tropical region, which was something she'd never experienced. Her homeworld orbited a red dwarf star that produced barely enough light and heat to allow the mining colonies established there to survive. She'd read about places like this, but until recently she had never expected to see one in person.

The air was sultry and what little breeze stirred

carried notes of blooming flowers, growing things, and water. If she'd come here as part of the tour, she likely would have enjoyed this place. As it was, she couldn't wait to leave. This world was full of unknown threats, and she had no way of protecting herself from any of them.

The thought of what dangers might be out there made the hair on the back of her neck rise. She lifted her head to scan the shore and then shrieked in surprise as something brushed against her submerged foot.

She jerked backward and tried to swing her feet out of the water. She almost managed it, but her robe was still drenched in the slick gooey gel and so was the float she sat on. She slid toward the water, her desperate attempts to find something to hang on to only making the situation worse.

Within seconds, she was underwater, arms and legs flailing in a desperate attempt to fend off any aquatic predator. Then she remembered she also needed to breathe and clawed at the water in a frantic attempt to reach the surface.

The robe weighed her down and slowed her movements, but she couldn't take the time to undo the knot and free herself. Her lungs burned by the time she broke through and could finally get her head above the water.

Air!

She sucked in several deep, desperate breaths and

looked around for the pod. It couldn't be far away. She'd swim over and find a way to pull herself back up.

Hope had to spin almost all the way around before she spotted it, and once she did, her heart dropped like a stone in high gravity. The pod had drifted far enough away that it wouldn't be easy for her to reach. She must have gotten momentarily stuck in a different current, or maybe her ungainly flailing had sent her pod sailing off in a new direction.

"Shit," she swore and looked around again, trying not to think about what might be in the water with her. Snakes? Fish? Giant reptiles who wanted to know what human tasted like? She needed to get out of the water. *Now*.

That's when she noticed the current wasn't pulling her in the same direction as the pod. She was now drifting toward a clump of rocks that jutted above the surface. It wasn't as safe as being on shore, but it was a big improvement over her present situation.

When she turned to look at the pod again, the distance between her and it had increased by an alarming amount. It might have had all the supplies she needed, but that wouldn't do her any good if she drowned before she reached the damned thing.

The rocks were closer, and once she'd rested, she'd be able to swim the rest of the way to shore. From there, she'd be able to follow the river and track her wayward pod.

Great, she had a plan. Or something close enough

to one to work for now. Hope aimed herself at the nearest rock and paddled toward it, painfully aware that at any second something carnivorous might decide she was part of the local food chain.

By the time she managed to clamber up onto the sun-heated surface of the rock, her adrenaline was spent. She curled her legs up so that no part of her dangled over the water, pillowed her head on her arms, and rested. Once she had her strength back, she'd swim the rest of the way to shore. And this time she'd leave the damned bathrobe behind if she had to.

3

————

It DIDN'T TAKE him long to reach his first destination. He'd explored every square meter of his territory and knew the fastest way to the river so well he could make the run blindfolded.

The only reason he didn't arrive faster was because he was on high alert. He hadn't seen any sign of the pod's occupants when he'd viewed the area from higher ground, but they had to be out there somewhere.

He assumed there was only one passenger, but that depended on the size of the beings on that ship and how desperate the situation was when they'd evacuated the main vessel. As much as he enjoyed a challenge, he had to be careful. If he failed, that would leave the rest of the clan exposed to danger. That couldn't happen. As difficult as he found it to spend time around his brothers, he'd willingly sacrifice himself to protect them. Especially if he took some of the enemy down at the same time.

After what the scrawnies had done to the fa'rel, they and anyone they hired had it coming.

Once he came within sight of the escape pod, he understood at least some of what had happened. The pod had drifted near the shore and gotten caught up in a snarl of driftwood and other flotsam. A careful check of the area revealed no footprints, freshly marked ground, or even a trace of scent. The chemical stench that clung to the pod and everything inside it would make it easy to detect if someone had come to shore here, but he saw nothing.

Whoever had been on board, they'd left before the pod reached this spot. Why they'd abandoned the pod and whatever supplies were on board was a puzzle for later. For now, he needed to make sure the invaders couldn't find the pod and recover their gear.

Menace waded out to the abandoned craft, examined it for a few minutes and then made a decision. It was too heavy for him to drag out of the water and into the trees to hide it. It would be much easier to sink it into deeper water and leave it to be recovered after the enemy was dealt with. The pod only had one seat, but that didn't mean someone else hadn't also been inside. It just meant they would have had a very cramped and unpleasant trip down.

He waded out until the water deepened and he couldn't touch the bottom anymore. Good enough. He didn't want it too far from shore since he intended to retrieve it later.

It didn't take long for him to pull the oblong-shaped vessel into position. Then, he got to have a little fun. He extended his claws and slashed the float to ribbons in several spots.

Air rushed out, frothing the water and making the whole thing spin until enough had escaped for the pod to sink. It vanished beneath the surface in a matter of minutes. Once the last of the air bubbles stopped rising, it would be impossible to spot from shore.

Perfect.

He'd spotted the most likely place for an emergency beacon to be housed before he sank the pod. Once it was underwater, it only took a few minutes, a knife, and several short dives to pry the panel off and cut through all the wires he could find. That took care of the beacon. Now, to find the pod's former inhabitant.

He made his way back to land, shook himself free of most of the water soaking his fur, and headed upriver to track down the enemy. They couldn't be far away. He'd find where they came ashore and follow their tracks from there. He couldn't imagine they'd be foolish enough to stay near the river. No one came to this planet unless they had the verexi's permission, and the only ones they granted access were those they'd hired to eliminate the fa'rel and erase the last evidence of their illicit experiments. Whoever they were, they knew they'd landed in enemy territory. If they were smart, they'd be taking precautions and making plans.

At least, that's what he'd do in their position.

When he found the enemy, he didn't know what to make of them. Instead of a combat-capable warrior, all he saw was a solitary being wrapped in what was either a white pelt or a bulky garment with no practical use. The enemy soldier was curled up on a rock some distance from the far shore, and from what he could see, they weren't armed. He wasn't even sure they were awake.

*It couldn't be this easy.*

He was sure of one thing now that he'd seen the enemy. More than one of them couldn't have been in the pod. There wasn't enough space inside.

That made his next decision easier. He removed the kilt and greaves and set aside the spear he carried. He checked the knives strapped to both biceps by leather thongs to make sure they were securely in place. He'd already taken off the leather shoulder sling he used to carry the spear and other items, but now he sorted through the contents until he found another useful item—a length of braided leather he used as rope.

While killing the invader immediately would let him indulge his violent side, capturing this person and interrogating them would be the smarter choice. He needed information, and that odd entity sunning itself on a rock would tell him all they knew before they died.

He left his possessions stashed between the roots of a tree and then made his way farther up the river before breaking cover. The enemy never looked up. In fact, they didn't move at all.

Still, he made his way to the water's edge with all of his stealth and skill.

Once he was in the river, he made sure to keep all but his head submerged to make him harder to see. Then he simply let the current carry him downstream. All he had to do was swim hard enough to keep his head above the water and make occasional adjustments to his course. The river did the rest.

When he was closer, he got his first good look at his quarry, and everything he saw conjured up more questions.

The white covering was definitely a garment and not fur. The enemy's hands and feet were bare skinned and many shades darker, and the hair on their head was brown and wavy. Why would anyone wear such heavy, hot clothing out here? Especially a mercenary? It made the wearer easy to spot and had to be cumbersome and difficult to move in.

This close, he was even more certain they had no weapons unless they had them hidden under their bulky clothing. In fact, they appeared to have no equipment at all. What kind of mercenary would abandon a perfectly good ship? If this was a trap, it was a terrible one. But if it wasn't a trap, what the fuck was the enemy doing? Taking a nap in hostile territory was a fast way to die. If one of the fa'rel didn't find them, the local predators would.

Especially as this mercenary seemed entirely unaware of their surroundings. They hadn't even looked up in the time he'd watched them. It was almost as if they weren't paying attention.

Of course, that was when the enemy finally raised their head to look around. Their gaze locked on to him, and he braced for whatever attack would come next. None came. Instead, they—no, *she*—sat bolt upright and screamed in terror.

He wasn't sure which of them was the most surprised, though she was definitely louder. He continued to swim toward her as his mind tried to make sense of what he was seeing. This was a female. The thick fabric had hidden her shape, but once she moved, the garment had fallen open, revealing the unmistakable form of a female—a human female. He'd seen them on the entertainment vids they'd sometimes been allowed to watch. That had to be what she was... but she wasn't like the ones he'd seen on the vids. She had the most stunning spots on her skin, patches of white that varied in size and shape. Some of her hair was pure white, making stripes in her hair.

She was beautiful. Why in the hells was she *here?* This was a prison planet in verexi space. It had to be a trap.

"Get away from me!" the female screamed and waved her arms, the sleeves flapping like soggy flags. "Shoo! Go away. I'm not on the menu."

He understood her, which meant that whatever language she spoke was programmed into his translator. That would make things easier. Still, he didn't say anything as he swam closer, waiting for the trap to close. If that's what this was.

She drew her legs under her and folded her arms across her middle while never taking her eyes off him.

When he was within a few meters, she spoke again. "Go away! I'm having the worst day ever and if you eat me, it will also be my last day. No one should die on their worst day."

She paused. "Though I suppose that's probably what usually happens. Death isn't often a good thing." The female uttered a broken sigh. "Still, I'd rather not die today, so fuck off like a nice monster and find something else to eat."

That did it. He curled his lips up in a snarl. "I am not a monster. No matter what those fucking scrawnies think."

The female gawked at him. "You can talk, and my translator knows the language you're speaking?"

He snorted with amusement. "Obviously."

To his shock, her expression changed from fear to embarrassment and remorse. "I'm so sorry. I didn't realize. You..." she gestured at him. "You do look rather terrifying from where I'm sitting."

"Why?" he asked, not sure where the question had come from or why he wanted to know. Maybe it was because she was the first person he'd ever spoken to who wasn't a verexi.

The question seemed to amuse her and some of the tension left her body as a ghost of a smile touched her lips. "You want to know why you're terrifying?"

"Yes." He allowed the current to push him closer to the rock she huddled on.

"All I can see of you right now is your head and shoulders. You're huge. You've got horns, fangs, and uh... stripes." She ran a hand down her forehead with two of her fingers mirroring the stripes that crossed his face from hairline to brow bone.

"I have no idea what race you are, but you're clearly not a vegetarian. Can you blame me for assuming you were part of the local wildlife and were here to see if I could be added to the food chain?"

It made sense. He still wasn't pleased she'd assumed he was a beast, but he had given her no reason to think otherwise. "I'm not here to eat you." He had intended to interrogate and kill her, but she didn't need to know that.

"I kind of guessed that when you spoke. I really am sorry I thought you were a monster." She huffed out a long breath. "I've had a very bad day. Did I mention that?"

"You did. And I want you to tell me about it once we reach the shore. This is not a good place to linger."

Her eyes immediately darted around, searching for danger. "It isn't?"

"No. A storm is coming. Lightning and water are a dangerous combination."

"A storm?" She looked up at the sky, which was still mostly clear. It wouldn't be for long. He'd seen the storm clouds gathering as he'd scanned the area, looking for the vessel he now knew was an escape pod.

"Soon. It's coming from that direction." He gestured toward the territory claimed by his clan.

She nodded her understanding but didn't otherwise move. He waited a few seconds and then swam up to the rock and glared up at her. "We need to go. Now."

"I..." she sighed, a mixture of defeat and embarrassment. "I don't swim very well. That's why I had to stop at this rock to rest instead of swimming all the way to shore."

He eyed her garment. "If you tried to swim in that thing, I'm surprised you made it this far. Remove it."

She stiffened and shook her head in short, jerky motions. "No."

A minute ago she thought he was terrifying, and now she was defying him? He'd made a mistake by being nice to her. He wouldn't do that again.

"Yes. You will. Now." He scowled up at her and then deliberately lifted one hand out of the water with his claws extended. "Either you remove that thing, or I will."

"It's all I have! I lost everything when I fell into the water. The escape pod drifted away with all my gear. I have no food, shelter, or anything to protect me from the storm you warned me about." She plucked at her still soggy sleeve. "This stupid spa robe is all I've got."

"And if you wear it while you're swimming, you're likely to drown before we reach shore."

She blinked at him in astonishment. "Aren't you going to help me?"

She thought he was here to rescue her? "First you thought I was a monster. Now you think I'm here to save you?"

"Uh. Yes. I mean, why else are you out here? This doesn't look like the nicest place to go swimming."

"It's not so bad." He deflected her question instead of lying to her about why he'd swum out to her.

"I guess. At least this means there can't be anything dangerous in these waters." She pursed her lips. "Apart from you, I mean."

He smirked. "Most predators around here know better than to tangle with me or my brethren." Then he pointed to the dark clouds that boiled up at the edge of the horizon. "The storm will be here soon. Decide now. Stay here or swim to shore."

"I'll swim. Can I have a second to get into the water and try something before we go?"

He growled with impatience but decided to allow it. "Do what you need, but do it quickly."

What did she wish to try? Was this the moment

she would attack him? It would be amusing to see this small female try something so foolish, but if she intended to try it, now was better than later.

He moved away as she clambered off the rock and into the water. To his annoyance, she kept the *spa robe* on. He had no idea what a spa was. Maybe he'd ask her about it later. Once she'd answered more important questions, like what ship she'd come from and what their intentions were.

Once she was in the water, she tried to paddle out of sight behind the rock. He followed.

"Um, can you give me some privacy?" she asked.

"Why?"

"Because I need to take this thing off to swim and well... I don't even know your name."

"Why is that important?"

"Because we're strangers!"

Her answer didn't make sense, but he could tell she was serious about it for some reason. "I am Menace, and I am not letting you out of my sight."

"Hello, Menace. I'm Hope. I have no idea why you need to watch me, but since you're my best chance of surviving this nightmare of a day..." She shrugged and then wriggled out of the robe, her head vanishing beneath the surface several times before she managed to get it off.

Then, instead of setting it aside, she wrapped it into a bundle and tied it with the belt.

Hope kept as much of her body beneath the water

as she could, but he now saw that both shoulders and the tops of her arms had more of the same spots as her face. The temptation to dive under the water and see how many more were still hidden from his view was strong, but he resisted. He'd be able to see more of her once they reached land.

If she tried to wear that thing in the forest, she'd get caught up on every vine and rock between here and his cave. He already had an idea of how to prevent that from happening. Even if his little prisoner wasn't going to like it.

**4**

_______

WHEN SHE'D FIRST SEEN the beast swimming toward her, she'd assumed it would kill her. All she'd been able to see were horns, striped fur, and fangs that peeked out from his upper lip.

She'd been certain it was a monster until _he_ had spoken to her. Not a monster at all, but a big, broad, fur-covered _something_ with horns, fangs, and claws that could slice her in half.

She swam behind him, doing her best to keep up but failing utterly. He moved his arms in long, powerful strokes that sped him through the water while she struggled to paddle along in his wake. The robe was awkward and heavy, even bundled up, and she struggled to keep it and her afloat at the same time.

He was halfway to land when he stopped swimming and spun around to check on her. She managed an awkward wave that nearly put her underwater again.

"You'll never make it that way." Menace swam back to her, covering the distance far faster than she could have. With a look of frustration, he pulled a length of something that looked like a braided rope over his head and held one end up.

"Catch this and tie it around your body. I'll drag you and that damned robe of yours to shore before we both get flash fried by lightning."

He didn't sound happy, but she smiled at him anyway. "Thank you."

He tossed her the rope. "You better be worth the trouble."

She caught the length of what turned out to be braided leather and did as he instructed. She didn't say anything because she had no idea how to respond to his last comment. Worth the trouble? Was he expecting to get paid for saving her? If so, he'd be sorely disappointed. Her wallet, credit chips, and everything else were still in her room on the *Bountiful Harvest*. Or what was left of it after it crashed.

"I'm ready," she said.

"Good. Keep your distance. Let me pull you. Your only task is to focus on staying above the water. Once we're ashore, you will not remove the rope. I don't want you running off."

Running off? Was he serious? Where in the nine hells would she go?

"I'm not going to run away. The way I see it, you're the best hope I have of finding my escape pod and retrieving my gear. Then you can be rid of me, and I'll wait for someone to fly down and rescue me and the other passengers."

"No one is coming here to rescue you."

"What? Of course they will. The ship I was on was registered and insured. Someone will come looking for us."

"Not here. This is a prison planet. The verexi ensure no one comes here unless they have permission, and the ones who have that also have instructions to kill what is left of my clan." He turned away from her, letting her see the scars that covered his back. White fur marked each of the lines something—or someone—had carved into the flesh, creating a crisscross pattern that spoke of terrible cruelty.

"P-prison planet?" she stumbled over the word.

"That's what I said." He swam as he spoke, pulling her through the water with apparent ease.

"But I haven't done anything wrong. My ship crashed. That's all. How can they make me stay here?"

Tears fell and she let them stream down her cheeks to blend with the river water.

His massive shoulders bunched in what she thought was a shrug. "We didn't do anything wrong either. But here we are, and here we'll stay until they manage to hunt us down and kill us, or we find a way to kill them."

Holy hells. She'd landed in the middle of some kind of war between the verexi and Menace's people. The story seemed familiar. She tried to remember what she knew about the race Menace called the scrawnies. They were an insectoid race with a vast collective intellect. Long ago, when they thought they were the only intelligent species in the galaxy, they'd engineered their race to be hyper-intelligent. As a result, they were physically weak to the point of fragility.

That was it! She'd seen several news stories and articles about something to do with the verexi creating an experimental species to act as their private army.

It was all top secret, of course, hidden from everyone including the verexi public until one of the specimens escaped. What was his name? Anger? Fury? Rage! Yes. Another violent name, just like Menace.

Rage had broken free with the help of a human freighter pilot. Later, they'd fallen in love and taken his story public in an attempt to force the verexi to free the rest of his kind.

She'd found the whole story noble and romantic, which was why it had caught her interest back then. Honestly, it had likely influenced her decision to go on this matchmaking cruise and try to find an alien hero of her own.

So much for *that* idea.

She'd somehow landed in the middle of the same story. Only her role involved danger and abject terror instead of heroism and romance. Instead of a handsome hero sweeping her off her feet, she had a big, growly alien towing her to shore on a strange world—a *prison* world. That didn't match what she's seen and heard on the news. It was supposed to be a refuge for Rage's brothers.

She recalled another detail—an important one. The transfer hadn't gone as planned. For some reason the fa'rel had rebelled at the last minute. They'd taken over the ship, the verexi had fired on them, and the vessel had crashed on the planet's surface. After that, the verexi had revoked all access to that system and refused to allow anyone, even Rage, to contact the survivors.

Now everyone aboard the *Bountiful Harvest* was trapped here, too. Menace was right. No one was coming to rescue her.

*Fuck.*

She stayed quiet for the rest of the swim, her head full of questions and her arms busy paddling to keep her head above water. She needed to talk to Menace about what she knew, but this wasn't the time. For all she knew, it would make him angrier... and that wasn't something she wanted to witness.

Menace switched from swimming to wading when they were still some distance from shore. She tried to set her feet down but found nothing beneath her but more water. She soon realized why.

Menace was *huge*. She'd known that on some level,

but now she could see it. He had to be well over two meters tall and he was built like his diet consisted of steel bars and hull plating.

He looked a lot like the pictures she'd seen of his brother, Rage. They both had the same curled horns and golden eyes. Their markings were similar, though Menace had a thick beard a few shades darker than his dark blond hair. It fell past his shoulders, the lighter colors streaked with darker shades.

His back and arms were both covered in a tawny gold pelt of short fur that was currently plastered against his skin. The scars on his back were easier to see now, and she noted the way they twisted and bunched. Whatever he'd endured, he'd been left to heal on his own. She wanted to offer to look at them for him and see if she could do anything to help break down the tissue and help ease whatever discomfort they gave him.

She might not be a doctor, but that was only because she'd never been able to do the practical elements. She'd studied medicine most of her life, but she'd never been able to practice it because of her condition. Like so much of her life, she had the knowledge but not the experience.

Once her feet touched the bottom, she tore her gaze off Menace and focused on picking her way over slick rocks and through other hazards she tried not to think too much about. Weeds tangled around her ankles, sharp stones hurt her feet, and every step involved coming into contact with a warm slimy goo that clung to her skin.

"It's like a mud bath," she tried to tell herself.

"Why would you deliberately submerge yourself in mud?" Mayhem asked, and she belatedly realized she had spoken aloud.

"It's supposed to be relaxing and good for your skin, but that mud was very different from *this*."

She looked up and nearly tripped over her own feet. Mayhem was almost clear of the water, which meant she finally got a good look at him... *all* of him. Her next words came out in a squeaky voice she hardly recognized. "Where are your clothes?"

He turned back to look at her and she squeaked again as she dropped back into the thigh-deep water to hide herself while desperately trying not to look at him. "Eyes front!"

He laughed and shook his head. "I'm not sure what that means, but it sounded like an order. I don't take orders from anyone, especially someone I don't trust.

"My eyes are going to stay on you until I'm certain you're not going to attack me the first time I look away. As for your first question, my gear is stashed nearby so it didn't get wet. Unlike you, my time in the water was planned."

"You are clearly having a better day than I am," she grumbled. "I bet you didn't even have to deal with your luxury cruise ship getting attacked and crashing today.

Now, will you please turn around and give me a moment of privacy to get dressed?"

"Your obsession with covering up makes no sense, but if it gets you out of the water, I will turn my back. If you try anything…" He trailed off, leaving the threat unspoken.

"I'll talk the whole time, so you know where I am."

"Good. Tell me about the ship that brought you here."

She counted to three before looking up. Menace had turned away, so she stood up, tugged open the loose knot she'd tied in the belt, and did her best to wring out the robe before putting it back on.

While she dressed, she told him about the *Bountiful Harvest*. How it was a civilian cruise ship full of females like her, not an enemy vessel. It didn't even have weapons as far as she knew.

She didn't dare try to undo the tow rope, so she did her best to ignore it. Once she was covered, she said, "Thank you. Now I'm ready. And you can stop threatening me. I have no intentions of doing anything stupid. If I run away, my survival time could be measured in hours. If I attack you, that time shortens to minutes or possibly seconds."

"If what you said is true, I suspect it would be seconds," he said. "Why were you on this cruise? What was the point?"

Oh boy. This was the bit she hadn't wanted to admit. Could this day get any more humiliating? "It was a mating cruise. Human women pay to be pampered, travel to a few planets, and get introduced to eligible males from compatible species. Hell, we even saw a few noncompatible ones. I'm not sure what they were after, but none of them were interested in me, so I didn't ask."

"Why would you pay to find a mate? Did yours die?"

"Die? No. I've never been married or mated. I haven't even dated much. I wanted to see the worlds and maybe fall in love with someone." She dropped her head, embarrassed. "That didn't happen. No one was interested in me. One of them told me I should be ashamed of myself for even trying."

"No one?" His tone was one of utter disbelief. "Were these males defective?"

"No." She pointed to the spots on her face. "They think I am."

"Then they are stupid," Menace declared and then glanced over his shoulder. He gave a light tug on the rope she still had tied around her waist. "This way. If we hurry, we can be under shelter before the worst of the storm reaches us."

The *worst* of the storm? That did not sound promising. "I'll do my best to keep up."

He didn't say anything else until they were both on dry land. He led her through a field of the flame-colored grass and into the trees while she did her best to look at anything besides him and his really great ass.

The grass was soft and easy to walk on, enabling her to keep up with him without too much trouble. Once they were under the vibrant orange canopy of the forest, he stopped and then turned to face her.

Despite her best efforts, she couldn't stop herself from indulging in a brief moment of appreciation for the vision of male perfection in front of her. And yes, he was big all over, from the thick trunks of his thighs to the broad planes of his chest, and everything in between.

"Um, aren't you going to get dressed?"

"In a moment. First, I need to do something about you." He drew a knife from where it had been lashed to his biceps and eyed her thoughtfully.

Hope backed up until the rope tightened and she couldn't move any farther away. The blade in his hand held all her attention, looking well-used and dangerously sharp.

"Don't hurt me." The words were out of her mouth before she knew it.

He scowled at her. "Are you going to hurt me?"

"No. Of course not. Not that I think I could if I wanted to, but like I already said, I have no intention of trying."

"I have no interest in harming you unless you give me a reason." He softened his voice and lowered the hand holding the knife.

"Then why are you holding that?" She pointed to the blade.

"To fix that thing you insist on wearing. It will slow you down as much in this forest as it did in the water."

"Fix it how?" she asked suspiciously.

"It needs to be trimmed." He twisted his hand around the braided leather rope, shortening it slightly and bringing him a step closer to her.

"You're going to use that? Um, don't you have something smaller and less lethal looking?"

He actually smiled. The expression softened his features and made the skin around his eyes crinkle. "This is the smallest blade I have. Don't worry. I know what I'm doing."

"You go around cutting the clothes off a lot of females?"

"No. You'll be the first."

"The first? You're not filling me with confidence here." Hope sighed and lowered her gaze. "But you're going to do it anyway. Aren't you?"

"I've never seen a female in the flesh before, so no. I have not done this before. Hold still."

He was beside her in a second, and the next thing she knew he had hold of her left sleeve. He cut through the seam at her shoulder, the tip of the knife so close to her skin it made her shiver in fear mixed with something else. Something she didn't expect. Anticipation?

This was insane. He'd never even seen a woman before, so whatever was going on, it wasn't attraction. Not for him. Desperation, maybe. More likely curiosity. They weren't even the same species, and none of this was part of any plan she'd made for her future.

It only took a minute for him to cut away both sleeves and drop them on the ground by her feet. Then he kneeled in front of her and raised the knife again.

"Whoa! What are you doing now?" she asked.

"Cutting this shorter so you can walk."

"Oh. Right." She crossed her now-bare arms over her chest and tried to relax. Not the easiest thing to do when a huge, naked, and insanely attractive alien was kneeling at her feet. "Don't make it too short."

The second the words left her lips, she wanted to take them back and replace them with something less inane and ridiculous. Of all the things she had to worry about right now, showing too much skin wasn't even on her list.

His only response was a low grunt. He made a cut just above her knee, pulling the fabric away from her leg as he worked.

"Turn slowly."

She did as he asked and turned in place, hyperaware of every movement as the knife trimmed away more and more of her only piece of clothing. The knife never touched her skin, and he never laid a hand on her except to move the fabric.

When he finished, he gathered up the trimmings and handed them to her.

That's when it happened. Her hand brushed his in

what should have been a brief and inconsequential contact... Only it wasn't.

She swayed forward, leaning toward him as he rose from the ground. Her admiration of his appearance changed to something else—desire. She wanted to touch him again. To stroke his fur-covered body and feel for herself whether his muscles were as hard as they looked. She craved contact and so much more. She wanted *him*. Without a thought or even a scrap of sense, she dropped the bundle of fabric and splayed her hands across his hard chest.

Whatever madness had taken over, it must have infected Menace, too. Instead of pushing her away, he made a low, rumbling noise deep in his chest. He gripped the belt of her robe and used it to pull her in closer as he bent down to nuzzle the side of her neck.

His fangs grazed her skin and she trembled in anticipation, her pussy suddenly wet with desire. Her clit throbbed and her breath caught in her throat. Not long ago, she'd thought he was a monster determined to eat her. Now she wanted to devour *him*. What in the nine hells was happening right now?

**5**

—————

*FUCK.*

This *was* a trap. It had to be because he had no other explanation for his response to Hope's touch. He'd even dropped his weapon in his need to get closer, to taste her skin and feel her body pressed against his.

His cock swelled and hardened so fast it was almost painful, and his entire body burned with need. He wanted to pin her against the nearest tree, tear off that damned robe, and then bury himself balls-deep inside her until she screamed his name to the sky.

He'd used the pleasure bots the scrawnies had provided their creations from time to time, but that had been mindless rutting that left him spent but unsatisfied. It had been an empty, physical act. Now he had Hope in his arms, and he understood what had been missing. Her.

She wasn't simply the bait in this trap. She *was* the trap, and she'd captured him with a single touch.

"Why?" He raised his head so he could look down at her and read her expression when she answered. He had to know. Not that it would change anything. Right now, he'd happily face death so long as he could fuck Hope before he died.

"Hmm?" Hope's eyes fluttered open to gaze at him with a dreamy expression, and he found himself enthralled by their strange color—green with a cluster of golden brown at the center.

"Why are you doing this? And what are you doing to me?" He reached up to tangle the fingers of one hand into the soft waves of her hair and waited for her answer.

"I... what?" she asked. Her brow crinkled in confusion and her teeth sank into the plump rise of her lower lip. "I'm not doing anything."

He looked down pointedly to where her hands spanned his chest. "Yes, you are. I want to know why."

She snatched her hands away as if she'd been seared by an open flame. "Oh! Oh my stars, I'm sorry. I don't know why I did that. I promise I won't do it again."

That was not what he wanted to hear. "That's the problem, little beauty. I want your hands on me." He grinned in sudden amusement. "In fact, I want to feel more than just your hands touching me. I want you. I will have you. But before I do, I want to know why this is happening and what it will cost me."

"You do?" she asked in wide-eyed bewilderment. "You want me? Because I'm feeling the same way and I have no idea why." She winced. "I mean, you're gorgeous and naked and, well, uh... yeah. What woman wouldn't want you? But whatever this is, it started when our hands touched. Boom. Insta-lust."

"You deny this is your doing?" He released her belt to palm her ass with his free hand, pulling her up against his erect and throbbing cock.

"It isn't! I swear." Hope raised her hands defensively. "I thought it was you."

"It isn't." At least, he didn't think it was, but there was so much they didn't know about themselves. The verexi had tried to create a fighting force to protect themselves, one that was entirely obedient. They had failed. The fa'rel were deadly warriors, but they answered to no one but themselves.

Not until today. Not until *her*.

"Then what is it? And how do we make it stop?" Despite her words, Hope didn't struggle or try to pull away. In fact, she touched him again, this time running her fingers along one curved horn.

"I don't know what this is." He leaned down until his mouth was almost touching hers. "But stopping is the last thing on my mind right now. I will ask you this once. Answer truthfully. Is this a trap?"

She exhaled softly and shook her head. "No trap."

He believed her. "Good."

Then his mouth met hers and words ceased to matter. Her lips were soft and sweet as he kissed her, and the low moan of need that rose from her throat made his balls ache and his cock throb. He slid his tongue across the seam of her lips, and she opened her mouth to him.

Heat seared through him as his tongue tangled with hers, both of them breathless and straining against each other. He couldn't get enough of her. The silken softness of her skin was addictive, her scent alluring, and her tiny form fit against him so perfectly he'd happily keep her in his arms forever.

*Forever.* He didn't do forever. He lived in the moment. As a prisoner it had been the only way to stay sane. Until today, he'd assumed his future would be the same as every other day on this world: hunt, sleep, and protect the clan. Repeat until he died.

Then he'd found Hope and now... Menace shook his head, as if that could somehow clear his mind of the strange new thoughts taking root there. All of them involved the little spotted female he held. He wanted to fuck her, protect her, and spend the rest of his life with her.

If this wasn't a trap, he was in serious trouble.

The lust fogging his brain didn't clear until the first peal of thunder boomed. They had to go. Now.

He kissed her again, despite the need to hurry. "Use the knife I dropped to cut yourself free of the rope. I need to retrieve my things." He waggled a finger at her. "And if you try to stab me with my own blade, you will regret it."

She rolled her eyes and gave him a look of pure frustration. "You have serious trust issues, Ace. How many times do I have to tell you I'm not stupid or suicidal? I'd like to live longer than the next few minutes." She threw out her arms. "None of *this* was part of my plan."

"You have a plan? You will tell me what it was once we are under shelter." He turned and walked away from her, deliberately leaving himself open to attack. Not that he thought she would. Not anymore. But if he was wrong, it was better to know now.

Nothing happened. He heard her move and assumed she picked up the knife, but no attacked followed.

He jogged back to where he'd left his things and geared up as quickly as possible. Being in the forest during a storm was safer than being out in the open, but it was still dangerous.

He never let his attention stray far from Hope. She did as he'd instructed and cut away the rope. She tried to undo the knot at first but quickly realized it was impossible. The knot had cinched itself too tightly, and the leather had soaked up too much water.

He noted with approval that she didn't discard the severed section, though. She coiled the longer piece and set it on the ground before using the shorter section to bundle up the fabric he'd cut off her robe.

Practical was good. She'd need to think that way to survive here. The equipment and supplies the scrawnies had left for his clan were not what they had been promised. It was no surprise to any of them that the rations were mostly expired, and the equipment was a strange mix of surplus items and junk. They had bathtubs and countless tools no one knew how to use, but very little in the way of power generators, batteries, or building supplies.

Of course, the fucking scrawnies had never intended for them to survive long enough to use what they'd sent. None of them could figure out why the verexi had sent anything at all.

He jogged back to her, making his way over the tangled roots and stones underfoot. Orange and yellow moss grew over everything, hiding unstable footing and other dangers beneath a soft carpet that promised comfort but often delivered unpleasant surprises.

"Watch your footing. Try not to fall behind." He gathered up the rope and knife from the ground, securing them to his body again. He hadn't meant to be so brusque, but now that he was close to her again, all he wanted to do was ignore the storm and take what he needed. She had him off balance in a way he'd never experienced before.

Was this what it was like with all females?

Something told him it wasn't. Hope was special. She was *his*.

"Where are we going?" Hope asked.

"Somewhere warm, dry, and safe from the storm. That's all you need to know."

Her shoulders sagged and her gaze dropped to the ground at her feet. "Okay."

He growled in frustration. Not at her, but at himself. He'd enjoyed her fearful reactions to him at first but not anymore. Now he wanted her to look him in the eyes and call him that ridiculous nickname. Ace was some kind of card used in human gambling rituals. At least that's the definition his translator had provided when prompted.

"I have a cave nearby. We'll be comfortable there until the storm passes."

She lifted her head a little, peeking up at him from beneath a fan of dark lashes. "You live in a cave?"

"I live in a house." He tapped his chest with two fingers. "Not a monster. Remember? I shelter in a cave sometimes when the weather acts up before I can reach my home. These storms are dangerous. We need to hurry."

He set off at a gentle jog, hoping she'd be able to keep up.

After twenty or so meters, it was obvious that she couldn't match his pace. Not even close. He stopped and turned around to watch her, trying to understand why she was so slow.

The answer was obvious the moment he took the time to look carefully. Her feet were too soft for the terrain. It didn't make sense to him. How could a person's feet be so tender? Did humans limp all the time? Or was this another element of their cultural need to cover up?

He tried to remember how humans had appeared in the vids he'd seen, but apart from their need to wear layers of fabric, he had never noticed their feet.

Hope kept moving despite her discomfort, her lips set in a thin, determined line as she limped after him.

"Stop," he called out.

"I'm fine." She tried to speed up and immediately stepped on something that made her stiffen and clamp her lips together even tighter.

He'd seen enough. "You are not fine. Stop moving. I will come to you." He'd witnessed more than his share of pain and suffering in his life. All of it involving his clan brothers. This was somehow worse. It took him a few seconds to realize that was because this time, he was in a position to do something about it. He wasn't a victim or a captive. Not anymore.

If they'd had more time, he would have instructed her to sit down so he could check and see how badly she was injured. Time was in short supply, though. Instead, he stalked over to her and swept her into his arms.

"What are you doing?" she asked, her voice as sharp as one of his knives. He couldn't tell what emotions made her sound that way. Feelings weren't something he knew much about. They were messy, complicated things best ignored. But he didn't want to ignore Hope.

This was definitely a trap. He just didn't understand what kind.

"You're hurting yourself and moving too slowly. This is better." He cradled her against his chest, gave her a brief second to settle herself, and then took off at a run.

Hope yelped in surprise and flung her arms around his neck, her face pressed against his shoulder as he vaulted over a fallen log without slowing his pace.

He sped up and tried to pretend it was to get ahead of the storm and not because he wanted to show off for the little female. He leaped over obstacles and dodged around trees, deliberately choosing a path that would take him over more challenging terrain.

Before long she stopped making little fretful noises and started to enjoy herself. She laughed and offered up encouragement, which only made him run faster.

The storm caught up to them when they were only a short distance from the cave. By the time they reached shelter, they were both soaked to the skin, but not even the deluge could dampen the fire burning inside him.

He barely slowed down until they were only a few steps from the cave mouth. He had to sink the claws of his feet into the ground to reduce his speed. He came to a stop near the back of the shelter and grudgingly set her down, letting her lean on him in case her feet hurt too much.

"Sit," he said. "I'll be back with a light and something to treat your injuries."

What he really wanted to do was to peel off her remaining garment, lay her on the nearest flat surface, and fuck her until he got his mind back. Instead, he went to get what little first aid gear they had salvaged from the wreckage of the ship that brought them here.

If any of his brothers saw him now, they'd fall down laughing at his sudden need to care for another person. For one brief moment he thought about risking the storm to take her to Bysshe, the only one of their clan who wasn't fa'rel. The android would know what to do with Hope. He could deliver her to the android and be free of her.

The idea of leaving her made him snarl aloud. He wasn't letting her go. Not yet.

A voice growled at him from the darkest part of his mind. *Not ever*.

**6**

———

Hope found a simple bench of hewn wood and took a seat. It stood higher than she was used to, but that made sense given that it had been made for Menace. The wood was smooth but not perfectly polished and she idly wondered if he'd made it himself.

The cave wasn't anything like she'd expected. The roof overhead was raw stone, but the walls were covered with roughly hewn planks as was the floor, giving the space a homey feel. At least, until she noticed what was hanging from the walls. Weapons. Lots of them. She'd been amused and horrified by the number of weapons Menace sported when he'd gone to gear up. Compared to what was in this cave, he'd barely been armed at all. He had blades of various lengths and styles along with several spears. Even a bow with a quiver of arrows hung on the peg beside it. Was this a place of shelter or an armory?

After looking further, she decided it was a bit of both. Some shelves held what looked like ration packs while others held tools and things she couldn't identify. Apart from the bench, the only furnishings were a small table and a bed of some sort against the back wall. It was hard to see in the dimness, but it had to be a bed, albeit a rustic one. More like a mattress laid out on the floor. Still, it was better than what she'd envisioned when Menace had mentioned a cave.

Her distractingly hot and distressingly growly host rummaged through the contents of several shelves. This time, he turned his back to her without threatening her first. She considered that an improvement. He'd undressed again, but at least he'd put away most of his weaponry. All he wore were two knives lashed to his biceps by bits of leather.

She focused on the knives. It was safer than looking at the rest of his big, buff, and very naked body. That way lay temptation, and she'd already learned that when it came to Menace, she lacked all control.

That worried her less than it should have. In fact, she found it difficult to worry about much at the moment. How had the other passengers fared? What about the crew of the *Bountiful Harvest*? What was she going to do if she couldn't leave this place?

She'd made so many plans over the years. Some simple, some grand. None of them included spending the rest of her life on a prison planet. So why wasn't she more upset? As far as she could tell, this wasn't a dream or a hallucination brought on by head trauma. Shock had plenty of symptoms, but none of them involved random acts of lust with aliens. At least they hadn't been mentioned in any of the training manuals she'd read.

Her mind leaped from thought to thought until Menace turned and walked back toward her, holding a light pod in one hand and a plastic kit marked with the verexi version of a red cross in the other.

The light source was the first high-tech thing she'd seen since she'd lost her escape pod. "You have power?" she asked and nodded toward the item in his hand.

"There's a small solar panel outside. It's wired to a single battery." He kneeled down, set the pod on the floor, and tapped it twice to activate it. "It's enough to keep a few of these charged up and ready in case I need them."

She barely heard a word he said. It was almost impossible to think with him sitting at her feet. The light made his eyes glow like molten gold, and she had to clasp her hands together in her lap to stop herself from reaching out to stroke his face.

"Let me see your feet."

It wasn't easy to lift her foot without making the robe gape open, but she managed it.

Menace cupped the heel of one foot in his big hand as he inspected her injuries. His touch was surprisingly gentle, and when he lifted his head again, he looked almost relieved. "You have bruises and scrapes, but no cuts. That's good. I'll dress this foot first and then see to the other. Are you hurt anywhere else? Infections are a serious concern here. We have almost no medications, and what we do have was created by the verexi to treat us. We have no human medicine."

"I understand." She almost told him about her medical training but decided this wasn't the time. He was doing his best to take care of her, and she didn't want to act as if she could do a better job herself. If only she hadn't gotten separated from the escape pod. There had to be a first aid kit among the supplies. If she was stuck here, she was going to need it—and anything else she could salvage.

He cleaned and dressed her injured feet, but once he was finished, he didn't move away. They stared at each other for what felt like forever, the silence filled with the hiss of rain and occasional boom of thunder. Her heart raced and every cell of her being cried out with need. She wanted him to touch her, to kiss her again. Hells, she wanted a lot more than that. She wanted him any way she could.

Intimacy was a rare thing when any contact could lead to sickness or death. She'd risked it a few times, but she had never wanted—no—she'd never craved sex like this.

Finally, he broke the silence. "You will stay with me." It wasn't a question but a statement.

Hope didn't know if he meant for the night or the rest of her life, and she honestly didn't care. "Yes."

That one word broke the big male's control and sent him surging toward her. His hands gripped her thighs, spreading them widely enough for him to fit between.

She barely had time to catch hold of his horns for balance before his face was buried deep in her sex.

His next growl vibrated against her clit and she cried out at the unexpected pleasure it unleashed inside her.

The burning need she'd tried so hard to ignore rekindled in a flash, searing down to her soul and burning away the last of her doubts.

For the first time in her life, Hope lived only in this one perfect moment. No lists. No future. No plans.

Raw pleasure washed over her, almost drowning her in a disorienting sea of sensations. She clung to him as he devoured her, every swipe of his tongue bringing her closer to the brink.

When she didn't think she could take any more, he slowed down, prolonging her pleasure and teasing her by circling her clit with the tip of his tongue. She tugged on his horns to bring him closer, but he was too strong for her. He laughed at her efforts, slowing down even more.

He raised his head slightly, his eyes fever bright and his mouth wet with her arousal. "Tell me what you need, little beauty."

She huffed out a laugh. "You know what I need."

"I do. But I still want to hear you say it." His voice was as deep as the thunder overhead.

"I..." She'd never been this brazen before, and she found it hard to say the words aloud.

"Say it!" Menace demanded.

"Make me come. Please. And then fuck me until I come again. That's what I want."

He grinned so widely she saw his fangs, and all she could think was that he really looked like a cat who'd been offered a canary in cream sauce. She decided not to say that out loud. Insults would interrupt orgasms, and no one wanted that.

That thought fled the moment his mouth caressed her pussy again. This time he used his fingers too, plunging into her channel again and again.

It was like being back in the escape pod again. She felt like she was tumbling out of control, only this time, instead of crashing into a planet, she was plummeting into a world of pleasure.

"Yes. Like that," she encouraged. "Just. Like... Yes!"

Her release hit as hard as the storm raging outside. She cried out his name as pleasure coursed through every cell of her being. Menace never stopped, his mouth and fingers continuing their work and taking her deeper into ecstasy.

When he finally withdrew his hand and raised his head, Hope hadn't yet got her breathing or her brain back under control. She expected he would give her a few moments to recover, or maybe suggest they move this to the bed.

He didn't.

He wiped his mouth with the back of one hand, locked eyes with her, and then deliberately ran his tongue over his knuckles. "Tastes like more."

She opened her mouth to speak, but nothing more than a thin squeak came out. Had he really said that? Aloud. To *her*?

She closed her mouth before her unfiltered and off-balance brain could fire off a comment about the cat getting her tongue.

"You have nothing to say?" he asked.

She drank in the sight of the male in front of her. Huge, alien, dangerous, and sexier than anything she'd ever imagined.

"I think we're a bit beyond words at this point," she said coyly.

Menace's lips curved up into the most predatory smile she'd ever witnessed. "Agreed."

A second later his hands were on his hips, and the moment after that he'd pulled her off the bench and into his arms.

They fell backward with Menace controlling their descent. The momentum carried her with him to the floor, throwing her forward so she ended up sprawled across his broad chest. She tried to sit up and get some of her weight off him, pushing down on his chest as she slipped her legs over his hips.

It didn't work out the way she intended. Instead of giving him space, she wound up with her pussy pressed against the hard bar of his cock, her legs spread on either side of him.

Her body pushed her brain aside and took control of the situation. She rolled her hips and ground herself against him, the thick head of his erection sliding through her folds.

Menace raised his head to watch her, his gaze so hot she could almost feel it sear her skin. He kept his hands on her hips to steady her, which was a good thing because her legs were too short to reach the floor.

At first, he simply held her as she teased them both with her movements, but soon his grip strengthened and he began to dictate the pace. His hips rose to meet her as she passed over the tip of his cock, increasing the friction between them.

When he lifted her into the air, she dropped her hands to his wrists to balance herself, feeling more open and vulnerable than she'd ever been before. He never took his eyes off her as he lowered her onto his cock and let her slowly slide down the thick length of it.

Ridges she hadn't noticed before stroked over her innermost flesh and she couldn't hold back a moan as they came together.

Menace's breath hissed out over his teeth as she took him all in and finally settled atop him once more. She flexed experimentally and felt a moment of power as the massive male beneath her closed his eyes and shuddered in pleasure. Pleasure *she* had given him. This moment was the culmination of everything she'd dreamed about through all her years of careful isolation. She'd found freedom, even if it took a very different shape than what she'd envisioned. It wasn't planned, and she doubted it could last, but for this one perfect moment, she was free to make any choice she liked.

She looked down at Menace and smiled. This was one choice she'd never regret.

The moment didn't last. How could it when the need to move—to ride his cock until she came—grew stronger every second?

She let instinct take over and leaned forward, planting her hands by his shoulders and bracing herself over him.

He raised his head to kiss her hungrily. One hand left her hip to tangle in her hair, using it to guide her head down to his. As she leaned forward, he snapped his hips up, pushing them both up and driving his cock even deeper into her body.

She surrendered control at that point, happy to let him take the lead in this wild dance. She kissed him with a passion that matched his, giving in to needs and desires she'd never known she had. Not until now.

Not until him.

His grip in her hair was tight enough to sting without ever crossing over into true pain, and each time their bodies came together she felt a delicious ache as his cock stretched her inner walls.

She flexed those walls around him and felt his body tense as a low curse tore from his lips. "Fuck. Yeah. Do that again, little beauty."

She did, and the next thing she knew, he'd released her hair and gone back to holding her hips. He lifted her higher, putting space between their bodies, as she whimpered in protest at the separation. But he was too strong for her to do anything about it. He could do anything he wanted, and she'd be powerless to stop him… but somehow she knew he'd never hurt her.

"Mine," she almost missed the single syllable he uttered against her mouth.

She almost protested that she wasn't any such thing, but that would require thinking and talking— neither of which was really possible at the moment.

He nipped at her lower lip as his hips slammed up in another powerful thrust. "Say it."

She couldn't do it. Sex with her rescuer was one thing, but what if this was a mating ritual for Menace and his kind? She couldn't promise him anything. She had so many plans, and none of them involved this place or him.

Instead of speaking, she kissed him again and hoped it would be enough. That she would be enough for him for this one moment.

He growled and rolled over, taking her with him and trading places so he was above her, his weight braced on his arms as he powered into her with hard, fast strokes.

She clung to him, her nails biting into his shoulders as he laid claim to her body in a pounding rhythm that matched the beating of her heart. Hard muscles flexed and moved beneath her hands, and his mouth was mated to hers. Each kiss flowed into the next, all of them wild and possessive.

This time her orgasm came on slower, leaving her panting and desperate to reach a peak she couldn't quite capture—not until his cock swelled, his ridges contacting the perfect spot to trigger release.

Her cries filled the cave as pleasure overtook her, only to be drowned out by Menace's primal roar. He emptied himself into her with one last thrust, and then they were somehow locked together, the ridges that had given her so much pleasure swollen to the point that even the smallest movement sent aftershocks coursing through her body.

She stayed where she was, her senses scattered like stars in the night sky. Menace lifted his head to smile at her, a surprisingly gentle, almost reverential expression that made her heart ache.

No one had ever looked at her that way before. It made her feel beautiful, and that was the one thing she'd learned she could never be. No male of any species had ever wanted her.

A little voice whispered that she was wrong about that. One male did. Menace.

## 7

He probably should feel bad for taking Hope on the bare floor of his cave, but Menace had no regrets. How could he when she'd given him something he'd never imagined was possible? He'd sated himself with pleasure bots when given the opportunity, but he'd never had sex with a living female before. Now he was locked inside of one, still reeling from the raw overload of pleasure he'd experienced.

If this was a trap, he'd die happy. That was more than he ever expected to achieve in his life.

His moment of happiness quickly evaporated. A burning sensation crawled over the skin of his chest, only to fade away before he could do anything but look down to see what had caused it.

He expected to see Hope holding a weapon of some kind, but nothing was there. A second later the little female uttered a small yelp of surprise and snatched back her hands from where they'd rested on his shoulders.

He couldn't pull away without hurting her, so he couldn't do anything from his current position. He made a mental note to plan things better next time. And there would be a next time. Soon. But first he needed to find out what had burned him and whether Hope was somehow involved. Years of suspicion made him think she was, but his heart was sure she wasn't.

His heart needed to take lessons from his head before it got him killed.

"I'm going to move us. You hang on and let me do the work," he told her.

"What was that?"

"I don't know. Give me a second." The last thing he wanted was to move right now, but he needed to. He rolled onto his back, careful to bring Hope with him. Once there, he sat up so they were face to face, their bodies still bound together.

Hope immediately raised her wrists to eye level. "What are these?"

Two sets of dark lines intersected over the top of her wrists, like something had clawed her and left scars. Only she hadn't had those marks a few seconds ago.

He shook his head, baffled. He didn't know what the marks were. He'd never seen anything like them before, but he could tell by her expression that Hope had no idea, either.

Her gaze dropped to his chest, and she uttered a soft gasp. "You. You have them too."

He glanced down and found she was right. Three parallel lines crossed his chest. Two sets of lines started at his shoulders and intersected in the center of his chest before continuing on to a point over his ribcage.

She touched one of the marks with her free hand, running a finger along the now-black fur. The contact made his skin tighten to the point his fur stood on end, like the marks were somehow more sensitive.

"It looks like you were attacked by something with massive claws," she murmured.

"So does yours." He tapped a finger on the back of the wrist he still held in his hand.

Her pretty face crinkled into a frown of confusion. "But I barely felt anything at all. It was sort of an intense tingle. Nothing attacked us. I don't understand how this is possible."

"I don't either," he confessed. "But that doesn't change the fact that it happened." He captured both her hands in his and drew them to the center of his chest. "Our marks are identical. That has to mean something."

Hope pursed her lips and looked from her marks to his. "It doesn't have to mean anything at all."

"I think it does." Despite the fact he barely knew this female or that her arrival would turn his life upside down, he wanted it to mean that the two of them were bonded somehow. That felt right.

"I don't. Do you know why?" She drew one hand out of his grip to point to one of the larger splashes of pale skin that covered part of her jaw and cheek.

"This is called Segmental Vitiligo. At least, that's the medical term. Growing up, most of the people I knew called it Miner's Motley. It doesn't mean anything except I breathed in too much Talium-6 and my immune system malfunctioned. That's it. There's no special meaning to them. No symbolic purpose. They're just splotches that most people find ugly."

He snarled, furious that anyone could think of his little beauty that way. "No. Not ugly. Beautiful." Menace ran the tips of his fingers over her cheek and down her neck, tracing the edges of the marks. "Like your skin is painted."

"Not many see it that way." He felt her skin heat beneath his touch as she looked away from him, focusing on something over his shoulder.

"Then they are idiots." He scowled. "And they are not here. I am, and I say you are beautiful."

Her lips quirked up into a tiny smile. "That's sweet of you to say."

He bared his teeth and growled softly before saying, "You insult me. I am not sweet."

To his surprise, she laughed. "You are. You say sweet things and then growl at me afterward as if that will change what you said. You're kind, too. You saved me even when you thought I might be an enemy."

He growled again and then sheepishly realized he

was doing exactly what she'd accused him of only a few seconds ago. "I am not kind or sweet. I am dangerous. Even my brothers know this."

"Why can't you be dangerous *and* kind?" Hope asked.

Menace's mind locked up, and he just blinked at her for a time. He had no idea how to answer her question. That was the way of things. Then he remembered the advice Rage had given them time and time again.

"Because you can't be both. Kindness is weakness, and the weak don't survive for long."

Hope leaned forward, cupped his face in her hands, and kissed him gently. "I don't know who taught you that, but it's not true. I'm not dangerous, and I survived this long. Do you know why?"

He shook his head but didn't speak. He wanted to hear her explain.

"Because the same illness that gave me these spots also destroyed my immune system. I only survived because other people did their best to protect me. I had to stay isolated most of the time. I couldn't go to school or play with friends as a child. My parents sacrificed so much to keep me safe, and the rest of the community helped."

"If this is true, how are you here?" Worry sank pointed teeth into his guts. "Will you get sick again?"

He'd kill anything that threatened to hurt his little beauty, but how could he protect her from disease?

They'd talked long enough that their bodies were no longer locked together, so he decided the best place to continue this conversation was in bed. She'd be more comfortable there.

"First, we move. Then we talk," he told her and then gently lifted her off him.

"You're avoiding the subject," she complained, but she smiled as she said it.

"Am not. You have no fur to keep you warm and the floor is hard. I would be a poor mate if I didn't see to your comfort." The word came easily to his lips. So easily he didn't notice what he'd said, but Hope did.

"Mate?" she asked.

"*My* mate. That's what these markings mean. You are mine, little beauty."

"You don't know that," she protested.

He ignored her as he got to his feet and then reached down to help her up. Once she stood, he remembered her sore feet and picked her up again.

"I'm not that badly hurt."

He growled and stalked over to the bed at the back of the cave.

She laughed and rolled her eyes but didn't protest again.

Once she was settled on the bed, he decided it was time to prove his point. She was his, and he would take care of her. He moved around the shelter, quickly gathering up some dried meat and fresh water.

Then he brought the bounty over to her and set it

down within easy reach. Once that was done, he stretched out beside her, the two of them lying face to face, his hand on her hip.

"Now, tell me about this illness."

"I'm not sick. Not anymore. Sanco is a mining collective. We all live and work there and take a share of whatever profits we make. A few months ago, the miners found a massive Talium-6 deposit. I had inherited my parents' shares, plus the ones they bought for me when I was born. I used that money to leave home and travel to one of the few human medical centers that could cure my condition. The others with this condition will all get the treatment. The collective will see to it." She smiled. "Now, do you see what I mean about kindness? That's why I'm still alive."

"Your life was very different from mine," he said as he stewed over what she'd told him. "No one was kind to us. Well, no one but Bysshe."

"Who?" She cocked her head in puzzlement.

"Bysshe. He's an android the verexi purchased. They tasked him with our daily care and education. They were afraid of us and used Bysshe so they didn't need to come close unless we were already drugged or restrained."

He paused, expecting her to have questions. He'd never met anyone who didn't already know the details of his life, because everyone he knew had gone through that hell with him. He'd give her answers and then return to the topic he wanted to discuss… their marks and what they meant.

"You suffered so much." She touched the top of her shoulder with one hand. "Your back. They did that to you?"

"As a punishment, yes."

She bit her lip and sighed softly. "That's not a punishment. It looks like torture."

"It was that, too. Though the scrawnies would never call it that."

"Because they made you and thought of you as property, not people." At first he was surprised at the clear, simple way she described the situation. Then his surprise shifted to suspicion when he realized he'd never given her that information.

"How do you know about that?" he demanded.

"It was on the news feeds. Back then, I was still stuck in isolation and spent a lot of time consuming news as a way of feeling like I was still part of things."

"It was made public? When? What do you know?"

"Wait. They never told you? Those scrawny bastards? They said they did!"

"Explain." He appreciated her opinion of the verexi, but right now he wanted to know more.

"It was a big story. About a year ago when one of your brothers escaped from that horrible research base you were all on. He told his story to the media, and the backlash was so bad that the verexi had to promise to release you." Hope frowned. "Sorry, I'm trying to remember it all. It was a while ago."

"Escaped? Who?" No one had escaped. Was she lying to him, or had the verexi been the ones to lie.

It had to be the verexi.

"Rage?" the way she said his name was more of a question. "I think that was it. He looked like you, but his hair was shorter."

Her words fell like hammer blows that sent him reeling.

"Rage is dead. They told us he died trying to escape."

"Then they lied to you. I saw him being interviewed. He was the reason the rest of you were sent here. The verexi had to agree to set you all up on a safe world so you could live your lives in freedom. That's what was supposed to happen. But then the verexi claim you killed the crew and tried to take control of the ship. You were shot down out of self-defense."

"Lies!" His voice was so loud it made Hope flinch and push herself away from him.

"Not you. Them. The fucking scrawnies. They never told us any of this. I thought... we believed..." He shook his head and then reached out for her hand.

"Rage lives?"

She wrapped her small fingers around two of his and nodded fiercely. "He is alive. At least he was a year ago. The verexi banned him from their territory and had him escorted to the border. Then they disappeared. No one knows where they went. It was a big story for a time. Everyone was looking for the two of them and their ship."

"What ship was this? Who is with him?" He'd never asked so many questions in his life, but he needed to know everything.

"His mate. A human woman. I don't remember her name. She operated the cargo ship that resupplied the base where you were held. Rage escaped and ran to her ship for protection. She rescued him and flew away."

Hope stopped and then cover her hand with her mouth. "Holy nukes and novas. I wonder if the same thing happened to them. I mean, the marks." She pointed to his chest and then to her wrist. "The woman said she'd fallen in love with him and they were mates. But what if..."

Despite his shock at what he'd heard, Menace couldn't help but be smug. "I told you that's what they meant. You and I are bound together, little beauty. You belong here, with me."

"Or you could come with me," she pointed out. "I mean once we figure out how to get off this rock."

"If we escape this place, my brothers and I will make the verexi pay for what they did to us. Once that is done, I will come back for you."

"Revenge? Really? And what happens if you die? Then what would I do? Spend the rest of my life trying to survive here alone? I thought you said if we were mates, you'd take care of me. Not that I need babysitting, but I'm pretty sure I lack most of the skills I'd need to stay alive for more than a day or so."

Well, fuck. He hadn't thought about that. All his life he'd only had one goal: to survive long enough to pay the scrawnies back for what they'd done. As plans went, it was simple, direct, and easy to follow. Or it had been until now.

Now he had Hope. More than that, he had *hope*—the kind that made him want to look forward to the future and think about more than simply surviving.

What the hell was he supposed to do now?

"I don't know," he said grudgingly.

Hope sighed and moved closer again. "Neither do I. None of my plans included any of this. Or you. So I guess we'll have to work on a new plan together."

"Together," he agreed. "But before we do that, I want to hear more about Rage and his escape." He deliberately shifted his hand down so he was palming the soft curve of her ass. "Then I will make you scream again. After that, you will tell me about the plans you had."

"I'll talk if you will. I want to know more about you, too."

"I will." Once again, he was grateful none of his brothers could see him now. It was bad enough this female thought him kind, caring, and sweet. Now she wanted him to *talk* to her.

This had definitely been a trap.

## 8

Hope wasn't ready to embrace nudity the way Menace did. She had no problem watching him wander around the cave in the buff, but a lifetime of societal conditioning had left her with a need to be decently covered at all times. She knew it was dumb. Hells, she might have drowned trying to get to shore because she didn't want to give up her tattered bathrobe. Eventually she'd have to adapt to her new reality, but she had so many changes to face that this one was way down her ever-growing list.

Menace was gone for the moment. He'd told her he needed to confirm no predators were around and advised her to stay inside until he returned.

She was curious to see more of this world she might well be stuck on, but not until Menace had made sure it was safe. For the moment, she was content to explore the shelter he'd made for himself.

Maybe it would tell her more about what kind of male he was. They'd talked last night, but most of it had been about her. He might be the first male of any species she'd met who didn't constantly talk about himself.

The cave had been made into a practical shelter with minimal comforts, but everything she saw was sturdy and functional. She made a circuit of the small space, noting that almost everything had been made by hand. It reminded her of home. Not that she'd had anything like trees or wood on Sanco, but the feel was the same. It was all simple, durable, and *useable* in a way she hadn't seen since she'd left.

That changed when she arrived at the last set of shelves set near the back of the cave. She'd expected to find more supplies or basic tools. What she saw instead were dozens of carved wooden objects. Some were animals of various shapes and sizes, mostly reptiles, but a few were bird-like creatures, too. She also saw faces among the collection, but most of them were figures she recognized as fa'rel.

*This must be his family.* Several of the figurines were grouped separately from the others, and she rose on her toes to get a better look. She recognized one of them, and her heart twisted in her chest. It was Rage. At least, that's what it looked like to her.

Did that mean Menace had carved each of these to remember those he'd lost? It had to be. She smiled softly as she let her gaze drift over the little figures.

She'd been right. He *was* sweet. Even if he did his best to hide it.

Judging by what she saw, he was talented, too. Careful not to touch the figurines of his lost brothers, she reached out to brush her fingers along the exquisite curve of a flower that looked a little like a rose. It was the only flower carving on the shelf. *Probably because of his deep disdain for all things plant related,* she thought.

The wood grain was silky smooth beneath her finger, tempting her to pick it up. She didn't. Menace had these hidden in the back of his cave for a reason. He probably wouldn't be happy she'd discovered them.

She had learned one thing about him in their short time together. He wasn't used to sharing his feelings—or his life—with anyone. He was even lonelier than she had been.

To pass the time until Menace returned, she picked up the few dishes from where they'd eaten last night and went about tracking down a source of water to clean them. As she scoured them with sand and then rinsed them off, she thought about everything that had happened since that first warning siren had ended her massage.

Worry about the others gnawed at the corners of her mind. Did the other escape pods make it? What about the ship itself? Menace had assured her that two of his brothers had gone after the other pods they had tracked along with hers. If they'd survived, they'd be with... She had to stop and think to recall his brothers' names: Mayhem and Strife. Such strange names, but he'd assured her they would take care of any female they found.

She hoped Rissa had made it and was in one of the tracked pods, but she had no way to know yet. The fa'rel had no communication network, so they'd have to meet up with his clan brothers before she'd learn anything.

That thought led to ones about her missing escape pod. The emergency beacon might still be sending a signal. If Menace was right, no one would rescue her or any of the others. All the beacon would do was let the verexi know survivors were on their planet.

That wouldn't be good.

She still needed to warn Menace about the beacons. She'd forgotten about so many important things since her lover had first touched her. Now she had her mind back—at least for the moment—she wanted to make a list of all the things they needed to deal with. She sighed. It would be a long list, and she hadn't seen anything in their shelter she could write on or with. Surely something in her pod would do the job.

Her stomach growled, reminding her of another reason she'd like to find her escape pod. It had all her food and other emergency supplies. Last night she'd eaten enough to take the edge off her hunger, but she'd been careful about what she ate in case it didn't agree with her biology. So far, she'd had no reaction, but it would be safer for her to eat the emergency rations for now. It was yet another reason she needed to track down her errant escape pod.

Her mind wandered as she waited, and soon she'd abandoned lists and other practical concerns to remember last night. Being with Menace had been incredible. She'd been free and almost wanton at times, and today her body ached in delicious ways she'd never known before. As sudden and strange as it all was, she didn't have a single regret. Well, not about Menace, anyway.

Despite the fact he'd apparently never seen a female before, he'd treated her with relative kindness and respect, even if he was brusque and bossy at times. None of her plans had included anything like her current situation, but then, she'd never dreamed of finding someone like Menace, either.

Since all her plans had gone down with the *Bountiful Harvest,* maybe it was time to make new ones. Maybe. It was too soon to be sure. She'd only met him yesterday, but between the strange marks they shared and a sense of unshakeable *rightness*, she thought it might just work out.

Menace returned to the cave with a handful of freshly picked fruit for her, which he set down on the table with a look of mild disgust. "You really eat this?"

"Fruit? Yes. Humans are omnivores. We eat a lot of things."

"But it's a *plant*." He poked one of the golden orbs

with a finger. "I only know this one because Bysshe ferments it to make liquor. It should be safe."

He had water dripping from the curve of his horns and his fur was damp and stuck to his skin.

"Is it raining?" she asked.

"No. There is a small waterfall not far from here. I cleaned up there once I knew the area was clear. I can take you to see it after you eat."

"That would be fantastic. I'd love to get the last of the river grit out of my hair. But first, breakfast. Thank you for bringing me these." She picked up one of the fruits and bit into it cautiously, letting it sit on her tongue long enough to be sure she had no immediate reaction. It tasted delicious, sweet and juicy, but she resisted the urge to devour the whole thing. She only took a few more bites before setting it down on the table again. "Now we wait a bit to see if it goes down well."

He scowled in concern. "You think I would poison you?"

"No!" she said. "I'm trying to be careful. Once I'm sure it's safe, I intend to eat my fill. They're yummy."

"Yumm-ee?" He gave her a puzzled look as he sounded out the word. "What is that?"

Right. Translators were incredibly useful, but they had their limits. Especially when it came to human languages. "Delicious. It tastes like I want more."

Menace growled low in his throat and gave her a heated look. "So do you."

"Didn't you just take a cold shower?" she asked and tried to ignore the way her cheeks burned.

"Maybe I should take another one," he licked his lips. "With you."

"You and me under a waterfall?" Her libido lit up like a small sun. "I mean... we do have some time before I can be sure the fruit is safe to eat."

He growled again, the sound making her insides quiver in the most delightful way. He prowled toward her, and she moved to meet him, entirely unafraid. She'd learned his secret. Menace wasn't a monster... he just liked to pretend he was.

She knew better. She'd never fall in love with a monster... but she might be falling for him.

As it turned out, they didn't make it to the waterfall for another hour. Once she was cleaned and dressed—again—they finally headed off to track down her escape pod.

"You made me these booties so I could walk," she complained as he carried her through the forest to a spot along the river. He assured her it would be the most likely place for her pod to be. He didn't explain why he was so certain, but this was his home, so she trusted him.

"I did, and you will walk once I decide it's time."

He gave her a frustratingly smug look. "It's not time yet."

She lifted her feet to look at her new footwear. They wouldn't win any fashion awards, but they were functional. Menace had placed several layers of tanned hides inside each sleeve from her robe and then somehow stitched them together into boots. They had to be tied in place around her calves, but they'd protect her feet well enough. At least they would if he ever let her walk on her own.

"Has anyone ever told you how domineering you are?"

"Wait until you meet my brothers."

She shot him an irritated look. "I bet they say the same thing about you."

"Probably," he agreed. "But they're assholes."

He said it so casually that she had to laugh. She'd seen siblings bicker, of course, but she was an only child and had no firsthand experience. Something told her if she stayed here, that would change.

Today's journey wasn't a mad dash through a storm, so she had more time to take in her surroundings. The trees had trunks so wide and thick their diameter had to be measured in meters, and the roots rose out of the soil in places. They looked like massive serpents undulating through the ground, the dark bark mostly covered by a thick carpet of orange moss.

The forest canopy was high enough to almost feel

like a second sky, with orange, red, and gold leaves closing over their heads and leaving the forest floor in flame-tinted shadow.

She twisted in his arms to get a better look at one tree they passed, its trunk split and charred. As she did, her hand brushed over the scars at the top of his back, making Menace stiffen.

"They still pain you." It was a statement not a question.

"Sometimes."

"I can't promise anything, but I think I can help. There are ways to soften scar tissue. If we can find my pod, there might even be a way to fix them quickly."

He stiffened again and turned his head to glower at her. "No."

"No? Why not? If I were in pain, I'd want it to stop." That's why she'd studied medicine in the first place. Because she wanted to help people.

"My scars serve a purpose. They remind me of what I have survived."

"You live in pain because you don't want to forget what they did to you?" She doubted he'd ever forget. None of the fa'rel likely would. That kind of trauma could fade, but it rarely went away completely.

"Pain is part of the reminder." Menace's voice was barely more than a low rumble now.

"The scars would still be there. You don't need to suffer to remember." She waited a beat before adding.

"That's why you carved the figurines of your brothers, even the ones you lost. Isn't it?"

He growled again, though this one sounded more like a sigh. "You saw those?"

"I did. They're amazing. You do beautiful work. Why are they all hidden away in that cave, Ace?"

"Not all of them are hidden. I've given some things to my brothers." A smile touched the corners of his mouth. "Usually as part of an apology for something I said or did."

"Mmhm. Could that be because you're also an asshole?" she teased.

In response, he snarled and flashed his fangs.

She laughed and for a few minutes silence reigned as she drank in their surroundings. She had so much to learn about this place and the male carrying her.

"Will you teach me about this world? All I know is its name and the fact we weren't supposed to be anywhere near verexi space. Hopefully some of the crew survived and can explain how we wound up here."

"This planet has no name," Menace said firmly.

"Actually, it does. It's the third planet in the Raihan system, so the verexi refer to it as Raihan 3. Didn't they tell you where they were sending you?"

"They told us very little, and most of it was lies. None of us knew anything about this place apart from the fact we could survive here. Bysshe suspects the scrawnies wiped some of his memories before we left the lunar base. He has gaps in his memory he can't explain. If he ever knew the name of this place, they took it from him."

"So he's a survivor too. Like you."

"He is our brother in all the ways that matter," Menace agreed.

"I hope your brothers like me. If they don't..." she trailed off, not sure how to finish that sentence. If she wasn't accepted into his clan, what then? Would he still want her? If he didn't, her life would likely be short and very unpleasant.

"They will like you too much. Which is why I am in no hurry to introduce you to any of them. Bysshe is the exception. We'll need his help to determine what foods you can eat." His nose wrinkled in disgust. "Especially the plants."

"That would be helpful. Though so far I've been lucky. Nothing has bothered me. Still, it would be nice to be sure."

"I will take care of you, little beauty. You know this already."

"I know you've said it, but I've learned that saying something and following through aren't always the same thing, Ace."

He rumbled something in protest, but she couldn't catch the words... if there were any.

Then, her attention was caught by a flash of sunlight on water. They'd reached the river.

"You still haven't explained to me why you're so

sure my escape pod will be in this spot. This river is huge with so many currents and eddies. It could be anywhere."

Menace paused before answering. "I know because it was here yesterday."

"You *found* my pod already? Why didn't you tell me? Wait, you said it was here yesterday. It could have floated away by now."

"It can't float anywhere. I sank it."

"You what?" Why had he done that? And why hadn't he mentioned it before now? She wanted answers, and she wanted them right now.

**9**

————

Menace didn't understand why Hope was so distressed. Nothing had been damaged, and he'd retrieve everything she needed in a few minutes.

"I sank it. At the time, I thought it belonged to a mercenary paid to kill me and my brothers. I disabled the beacon, too."

She wasn't appeased by his explanation. In fact, she seemed more irritated than ever. "My food and supplies are all there, and you didn't think I needed to know?"

He huffed out a laugh. "The way I remember yesterday—once we got to shore, neither of us did much thinking."

That seemed to calm her. At least he saw her smile a little. "That's true. But still, mister broody loner out in the woods, you need to work on your communication skills." She nuzzled his cheek with hers and then dipped her head to whisper in his ear. "You're not alone anymore."

Her words flew like a spear thrown straight into his soul. Despite how much he cared for his clan brothers, he couldn't spend too much time in their company or he'd lose control of his darker side. That hadn't happened with Hope. He'd spent hours with her, even slept with her in his arms, and he was still calm and content. In fact, he felt happier than he could remember feeling. It was strange, but his little beauty soothed him in ways he couldn't understand.

Lacking the words to express what he felt, he kissed her instead. He moved slowly, savoring the soft sounds of arousal that rose from her throat as he nibbled and sucked on her lower lip. Traces of the fruit she'd had for breakfast lingered on her lips and tongue, but he didn't mind the taste anymore. They were part of her, and he craved her more than his next breath.

"Mine," he said when he finally raised his head.

She looked up at him with a dazed expression. "Mhm. Yours. Keep kissing me like that, Ace, and I'm totally keeping you forever."

"As my painted beauty wishes." He stroked over one of the pale patches on her cheek and then let his hand move into her hair to coil a lock of pure white hair around his fingers.

"Your painted beauty wishes to have a real meal soon." She leaned her head against his hand. "So, it's time for you to go swimming. I still can't believe you sank it. I mean, I get that you thought I was your enemy, but it's full of supplies and equipment you could have used."

"Which is why I stashed it somewhere I could find it again. The electronics are likely ruined, but that's a small price to pay to make sure the enemy couldn't find it and use what was inside."

She smirked a little. "You might be a little bit paranoid."

They'd reached the shoreline, and he set her on her feet before he responded to her statement. "I was a prisoner most of my life. It's not paranoia. It is caution and the reason I'm still alive."

Hope considered that for a moment and then nodded. "Fair point. Following that logic, I'm now going to try a little caution of my own and ask if there's any chance something will try to eat me while you're diving for sunken treasure."

That was a good question. "Yes, that's possible, but I have a solution." He scanned the area, looking for what he needed—a sapling on the edge of the woods, slender and straight enough for what he had in mind. He gouged a wedge out of one end with one of his knives and then flexed it at that point until it snapped.

He took a few more minutes to trim off the branches and cut it down to size to fit her smaller form and then used the blade to sharpen the thinner side into a point.

"Now you have a weapon. If anything tries to eat

you, you stab them with the sharp end." He handed it to her and showed her how to hold it.

"How will I know which animals are dangerous?" she asked.

He grinned. "They all are."

"Wonderful." Hope hefted the makeshift spear. "Try to be quick. Okay?"

He kissed her worry-creased brow. "I will be back very soon. It's just there." He pointed to the spot where he'd sunk the pod.

Hope lifted the spear to get a better look at it. "Would you carve some designs into this later on? Like those flowers I saw on the shelf."

Her request made his chest swell with pride. "As my beauty wishes."

She looked pleased, and that made him feel even better. He unslung the bag he was carrying and set it down beside her. Inside were a few tools and several lengths of rope. He hoped he wouldn't need them, but had decided to come prepared.

He instructed Hope to take a seat on a large rock near the water's edge. He watched approvingly as she settled herself with another, larger rock at her back. She had a good view of the area, both the river and the shore. She'd be fine for the short time it would take him to retrieve the equipment.

He waded in a few steps, but as soon as he was deep enough, he dove and swam hard for the sunken pod. It was exactly where he'd left it, and he flashed

Hope a smile and a wave before ducking under the water again.

It took several dives to find the latch, even though Hope had told him it would be at the back and near the bottom of the craft. The storm had increased the river's flow and stirred up sediment, making it harder to see.

Once it was open, he tried to haul the first container out, but it weighed more than he expected and he had to return to the surface for another breath before he tried again.

"I got it, but it's heavy," he called to Hope. "I'll be under a bit longer this time."

She nodded and poked her thumb up in what he assumed was a gesture of acknowledgment.

He took several deep breaths while enjoying the sight of her perched by the shore, spear in hand. His little beauty was adapting to her new situation surprisingly well. He would help her every way he could and protect her from the things she was too small to face on her own.

With that thought, he took in one last breath and went under. He had work to do.

The first container was too heavy to swim with, so he walked it across the river bottom as far as he could before coming up for air. Then he went down and repeated the process. It didn't take long until his head was above water and he could lug the container to shore without the need to be underwater.

Hope bounded to her feet and scampered over to

help him. She was making excited noises and grinning as they pulled it onto dry land.

The moment he set it down, she dropped to her knees beside it and unlocked the container.

"Yes!" she crowed excitedly once she had it open. "This is exactly what I wanted. Food, medical supplies, filtered water, and even some survival gear. I had no idea there'd be so much! Getting all this back to the cave won't be easy."

"And there's another container still inside. You said it was an inflatable shelter?" he asked.

"That's what the pod's computer said. It listed all available supplies several times during the descent. It should be in the same compartment as this one."

"Then I'll be back shortly with the shelter." He made a point of gesturing to her spear, which currently lay forgotten on the ground beside her. "Back to your post until I'm on shore again."

"Oh. Right!" She clambered to her feet, picked up her stick, and headed back to the rock she used as a seat. "Don't you need more time to rest before you go?"

He flexed his muscles and laughed. "Rest? No. But once we're back at the cave, I'll want to spend some time under the waterfall again." He let his smile turn wicked. "Care to help me get the silt and sand out of my fur?"

Her eyes gleamed with sudden hunger. "I think that can be arranged."

His cock began to stiffen and he let her see how much he liked that idea.

She laughed softly, gave his erection a knowing look, and then gestured to the water. "Enjoy your swim. I hope the water isn't too cold."

"I will take that as a challenge. Upon my return, I'll show you how little effect cold water has on me." He didn't wait to hear her reply. He had a job to do and the faster it was done, the sooner he'd be back on shore and balls deep inside his little beauty.

He dove into the water as soon as it was deep enough and swam hard for the spot above the escape pod. Determined to do this as quickly as possible, he sucked in three deep breaths and dove for the wreck, his arms and legs working to propel him down to the riverbed.

The sediment still hadn't settled from his last retrieval, and his movements stirred up the bottom again, leaving the water even murkier. He could make out the general shape of the pod, enough to know where to go. When the grit started to sting his eyes, he closed them and went by feel, confident he'd have no trouble. He wanted this over and done so he could get back to Hope.

He found the open hatch easily enough and got a grip on the edge of the opening. Then he reached inside and fumbled around for the handle of the second container.

When his fingers brushed against an extrusion, he

grabbed it and pulled, expecting to meet resistance as he hauled the thing through the hatch. Instead, his hand exploded with mind-searing pain. It felt as if his fingers had been stabbed with red-hot needles.

He pulled his arm out and planted his feet on the smooth, curving hull of the pod. Then he pushed off and swam for the surface, though he could only use one arm. The other hung at his side. The arm felt heavy and sluggish, but the pain hadn't lessened. In fact, he was certain it was worse.

He broke the surface, groaned, and then sucked in a fresh lungful of air as he struggled to lift his hand out of the water so he could look at it. What had injured him and how?

The answer was still in his hand, or rather, the remains of the creature clung to his hand. He'd crushed it in that first squeeze, but the damned thing had gotten its revenge. Even in death, it still pulsed and fluttered, trying to pump more of its venom into his body through the stingers still embedded in his skin.

He pulled one of his blades free from the ties that held it to his arm and used it to scrape the dead creature off his hand. He flung the brilliant blue and pink carcass far out into the river and then tried to swim for shore.

His hand throbbed and his stomach churned as if he was going to be sick, but that wouldn't be the worst of it. He'd been there when Shatter had encountered one of these creatures during their first weeks on the planet. His brother had died less than a day later, racked by pain, nausea, and delirium. They'd done all they could, but the crashed ship's medical unit hadn't been repaired yet. He was buried on the hill beyond the crash site, the first of them to die here but not the last.

Hope was hip deep in the water by the time he reached shore, her hands outstretched and her eyes wide with concern as she rushed to help him the rest of the way.

Dizziness made it difficult for him to walk, and by the time they reached dry land, she was supporting more of his weight than he'd have thought possible.

She somehow got him into the shade at the forest's edge, and then they were both on the ground. He didn't remember lying down, but that's where he was now, flat on his back with Hope kneeling beside him.

"What happened?" she asked.

"Local water creature. Bright colors. Squishy. Venom..." He nodded to his swollen and discolored hand, which she cradled in her smaller ones. "Dangerous."

"I can see that." She examined his injuries with deliberate calm. "Do you know how dangerous?"

He knew what she was asking. He didn't want to say the words. Didn't want to admit that his stupid need to hurry would cost him everything. He'd had one day with Hope. It hadn't even been a full day yet, and now he was dying.

It wasn't fucking fair.

He placed his uninjured hand over hers and stared into her worried eyes. "You need to tell the others about Rage and all the rest. They need to know. I have flares in the cave. When you get back, fire off one each hour until one of the others comes. Tell them to take you to Bysshe."

"What? No! I'm not leaving you here. You need help."

"No help. This..." A wave of dizziness hit and he had to wait until it passed before he could speak again. "This is how my brother died. Tell them to bury me by Shatter." He managed a weak smile. "But not too close. I still need my space."

Water spilled from her eyes to track down her cheeks, and she fixed him with a stare that would have made him find some other place to be... if he could walk.

Her next words came out with a low growl that made her sound like she was fa'rel. "Bullshit. No one is burying you anywhere." She glared at him and then gently placed his injured hand on his chest. "Do *not* move. Do you hear me? No moving. No dying. None of that. I will be right back, and you'd better be exactly where I left you."

Menace watched her rise with bewilderment. What had happened to the sweet, gentle female he'd rescued yesterday? Was this another side effect of the poison? Was he hallucinating?

He wasn't sure what was happening, but he decided it would be best if he didn't move. This new, growly version of Hope probably didn't exist outside his mind, but if she did, he'd be smart to do as she said. He was in enough pain already.

**10**

———

AFTER THE CHAOS and terror of yesterday's events, Hope had been enjoying the relative peace and quiet of today.

Too bad it didn't last.

One second she'd been sitting on a rock and admiring the lush beauty of this place. Menace's home was so different from the gray, dusty world where she'd grown up. That had been a grim, cold place where life was hard and nothing survived beyond the protection of the domes. Here, the air was warm and sweet, and life flourished everywhere. Despite the challenges and dangers, maybe she could build a life here. Maybe this was where she was needed, even if it wasn't what she'd thought she'd wanted.

Those warm, comfortable thoughts were shredded the moment Menace broke the surface. She could tell right away something was wrong. She dropped her spear and waded into the water, vaguely aware that if he'd been attacked by something, she was putting herself in danger with every step she took.

She didn't care.

As alarming as it was to see this big male weak and dizzy with pain, she didn't hesitate. She knew what to do. She'd studied medicine for years, and now all that information flowed through her mind, listing off the steps she had to take and the items she'd require.

Her only moment of panic came when Menace mentioned dying. That wouldn't happen, but if he thought it was inevitable, that belief might kill him. People could survive impossible odds if they were strong and stubborn enough not to let go, but that blade had two edges. If someone truly believed they were going to die... they died. And stars above, Menace was stubborn enough to do that to himself.

Once she'd laid down the law with Menace, she hurried over to the supplies he'd managed to bring ashore. The computer had recited the supply manifest several times on the way down, and she was certain it had mentioned a med-kit. Not a basic first aid kit, but something more robust. Hopefully, it had what she needed to help Menace, but if it didn't, she'd figure something else out. She had to. She needed him to stay alive. She didn't know the word for what they were to each other, but that didn't matter right now. They'd figure that out later. Once he was healthy again.

She let out a whoop of excitement when she finally

found what she was looking for. It was labeled as first aid, but it was large enough to hold more than the basics. She snagged a pack of sterile, filtered water in one hand, the kit in the other, and made her way back to Menace.

He hadn't moved, but he watched her through heavily lidded eyes as she approached. Thank the stars, he was still awake. She needed him to help her with this next bit.

"How bad is it? Scale of one to ten and do not pretend it doesn't hurt. I need to know the truth." She dropped to her knees beside him and tore open the water packet.

He gave her a sour look. "Fa'rel don't acknowledge pain. Pain means weakness and weakness means death."

She glared down at him. They didn't have time to deal with his pride or his past trauma. "This fa'rel better acknowledge what is very fucking obvious, so I can help him get better. I'm not your enemy, Ace." She used the nickname she'd given him and then raised her arm to show off her marked wrist. "I'm yours. Remember?"

His eyes opened wider, and a smile lifted the corners of his mouth. "Mine. My little beauty. I'm sorry to leave you so soon. Wanted more time."

She blinked away the tears that threatened to fall. This wasn't the time. She'd cry later, when this was over and he was well again. "We have all the time in the world. You just need to stay with me. Don't leave me here alone. If you do, who will protect me?" She threw out a challenge she knew he couldn't ignore. "Which of your brothers do you think will take me in?"

He snarled and bared his teeth. "None of them would dare!"

"If you die, I'll be alone here. I won't survive long without help."

"Bysshe will protect you," he stated, but she saw a flicker of doubt in his eyes that quickly turned into fierce determination.

"Maybe," she agreed.

He spouted a string of curses so fast her translator only caught a few of them, but it was enough for her to know her gambit had paid off.

"Heal me," he demanded, his voice a little stronger now.

"As my lover wishes," she replied. "But I'm going to need your help. If I show you some medications and read out the names, would your translator help you recognize them?"

"There's only one way to know." The fingers on his good hand twitched, but he remembered not to move. "Try it."

It took a few minutes to sort through the kit's contents. She stripped off her bathrobe and laid it out on the ground so she had somewhere to put everything. She couldn't be certain, but it looked like she had everything she needed. At least, she would if Menace recognized any of the medications and could confirm they were safe to use on him.

She opened the packet of water and handed it to him before carefully applying a pressure cuff to his forearm, restricting the flow of toxin into the rest of his body. "Drink at least half of that. Then we'll begin."

He chuckled weakly. "Now you sound like a fa'rel. Do this. Don't do that. What changed?"

She had to think about that for a moment while he drank the water. By the time he finished, she had an answer. "This is what I've always wanted to do. Heal people. Help them. I studied medicine for years, but I could never be certified because it wasn't safe for me to do the practical side of things. Someone with almost no immune system can't be around sick people." She shrugged. "But here, it doesn't matter. I can do this. I can help you. I can finally be *useful*." And there it was—the truth, revealed at last. She'd never found the words until this moment, but now it all made sense.

Every choice she'd made, every plan and list she ever wrote down, all came down to one thing. She needed a purpose.

Menace reached out with his good hand to touch her cheek. He didn't say a word, but his eyes held a deep understanding that untied the knots in her soul. She'd finally found her purpose. She was supposed to be here with Menace, taking care of his clan and any other survivors.

"Okay, let's do this," she said and held up the first

vial. "I'll read the name and you tell me if you recognize it. Hopefully, we can use something in here."

It turned out he knew several of the meds were safe for his species because they'd been part of the basic medic training they'd all received during their time with the verexi. In less than twenty minutes she had him dosed up with healing accelerants and pain relief meds. She'd cleaned up the site of the stings with sterile water and an antibiotic ointment. The ointment might not help, but she decided it couldn't hurt, either. She'd dressed the wound with a light wrapping of bandages to keep it free of irritants and then checked to make sure the pressure cuff was still doing its job. It was programmed to alter the amount of pressure exerted so that the limb was never completely starved of blood.

She let him rest while she tidied up and returned everything to the kit. Then she slipped away to grab more water and some food packs, along with two heat-conserving blankets she'd found. Then she sealed the container again and dragged it close to where Menace rested.

Once that was done, she used it as a bench to sit on while she packed everything inside the pouch Menace had worn slung over one shoulder. She had to tie a knot in the strap to shorten it. Otherwise, the bag banged into her knees with each step, but now it worked well enough. It would be best if they could stay here until he was stronger, but she wasn't sure the predators that roamed these woods would give them that time.

Once she had herself organized and dressed in her rapidly disintegrating robe, she moved to sit beside Menace. He was dozing fitfully, but when she took his good hand in hers, he twined their fingers together and squeezed.

"Just rest. If anything changes or you need food or water, you tell me," she said softly.

He cracked open one eye and she could swear he looked confused and surprised. "You will stay with me?"

His question had so many layers she didn't know where to start, so she simply smiled and nodded. "I'm not going anywhere without you."

He grunted in acknowledgment and closed his eyes. She knew he didn't trust easily, but he believed she'd watch over him while he rested. That was a gift she wouldn't forget.

She stayed with him in the shade of the trees, bathing his head and chest with water when he got too hot, though it seemed to be due to the weather and not a fever. She drank her fill of water and even ate one of the self-heating meals from the supplies. That turned out to be a mistake.

The scent of heated food carried on the wind as she wolfed down the contents, and the first signs of trouble arrived before she'd even finished her meal. A reptile of some sort hopped out of the trees to watch her with beady, black eyes. It didn't look overly dangerous. In fact, it was only a little bigger than knee height and its claws were too small to be a threat. Still, she didn't like the way it looked at her or the way its tongue flickered out past its small tusks to taste the air.

Cursing softly, she set down the food packet and picked up the spear Menace had given her. *Just in case.*

The thing chittered and hopped away when she moved, and for a moment, she thought it would go away. Instead, two more of the damned things appeared, and she heard rustling in the underbrush, indicating there were more she couldn't see.

"Menace, wake up. We have company. The kind that thinks we're on the menu," she hissed and squeezed his hand with quick, sharp motions she hoped would rouse him.

His breathing changed and his grip on her fingers tightened, but he didn't open his eyes. "Tell me what they look like."

"Small. Tusks. They make this chittering noise and hop around a lot. I think they came when they smelled the food I made for myself."

"Tusk-hoppers," the name sounded innocuous, but something in his tone made the hair on the back of her neck stand up. "Pack hunters. They are opportunistic hunters. Usually they'd be no threat, but now..." He sighed. "They are venomous, so keep your distance."

"We need to move away from them. Will they follow us?"

"Unlikely. They're opportunistic. The scent of food attracted them, and they're sticking around because they think I might be weak enough to take down. They won't chase us." He paused and then added. "Far."

He hadn't moved yet, but she got the sense he was about to. "What do I do?"

"When I stand up, give me your spear and then run. Do you know your way back to the cave?"

"I think so." She'd done her best to notice landmarks that would help her find her way, but she'd only gone this way once.

"I will tell you which way to run. Don't stop until I tell you to."

"Okay. When do we—

Before she could finish asking the question, she had her answer. Menace lunged to his feet with a roar that seemed to shake the trees and sent the pack of tusk-hoppers running.

She placed her spear in his good hand, turned in the direction they'd come, and ran. After about a hundred meters, Menace ordered her to stop. She slowed to a walk and looked back to see him loping up behind her. His injured arm was pressed to his body and his gait wasn't as steady as she liked. Still, he looked better than she felt. Weeks of rich food and minimal exercise were no way to prepare for a life-or-death flight through an unfamiliar forest.

"Do not move," he told her once they were close enough to talk quietly. He scanned the area carefully, turning in a slow circle until he faced her again. "They haven't followed us."

"Good." She saw him sway and rushed over to his side. She drew his injured arm carefully over her shoulders and leaned into his side to support him. "Can you keep going, or should we rest?"

"We should keep going, just to be sure." He looked down at her with amusement. "Though not for long. I don't think either of us is up for another run right now."

She stuck her tongue out at him. "Are you saying I'm out of shape?"

"I never said that. I like your shape." He leered at her, a sure sign he was on the mend.

"Good answer," she said, and let the matter drop.

It took them more than two hours to get back to the cave. They moved slowly and had to take frequent breaks because of Menace's weakened state. He never complained, though she knew he was in pain and unsteady thanks to both the toxin and the drugs in his system. He needed more rest than their situation allowed, but stopping for long put them both at risk. They pressed on. The booties he'd made protected her feet to a point, but they weren't perfect. Once she'd seen to Menace's injuries back at the cave, she'd have to tend to her own, too.

By the time they reached shelter, they leaned on each other for support, both of them limping and sore. The second Menace had the door in place, sealing them safely inside, she shooed him to bed.

"You need to rest. The more you sleep, the faster you'll heal."

He grumbled and tried to argue, but she didn't back down, and he was too tired to protest for long. To her relief, he fell into a deep sleep mere minutes after he lay down on the mattress at the back of the cave.

She grabbed another meal packet from the bag, barely waiting until it had finished the self-heating cycle before she tore it open and devoured the contents. She had no idea what flavor it was supposed to be, and honestly didn't care. It was food, and that was all that mattered.

Once she'd seen to his needs, she washed up as best she could, stripped off her ratty robe, and joined Menace on the bed, bringing the med-kit and several glow-pods with her.

She removed the bandages to examine his hand, which looked less swollen now. His breathing was strong and regular and so was his pulse. All good signs.

Once she was certain he was on the mend, she gave him another round of injections for pain and healing. With any luck, they were the last ones he'd need, but she made sure she had enough for more doses in case he required them.

Then she removed her makeshift boots and tended her feet. Yesterday's scrapes were healing, but the soles of her feet were swollen and bruised. Still, bruises healed fast, and the skin wasn't broken anywhere new, so she had no risk of infection. She took two anti-inflammatory tablets and set about putting everything back in the kit.

That's when she noticed a sealed item tucked into a corner, almost buried beneath the bandages and other items she'd stacked on top of it. The shaped seemed familiar. Was that...

She snatched it up and tore it open. Yes! It was a portable dermal regenerator. She checked it and confirmed it was fully charged and ready to go.

She tested it by using it on her feet first. After a few minutes, the swelling was markedly reduced, and the bruises were already starting to fade.

Pleased, she used it on Menace's hand next. It worked perfectly. By the time she was done, his fingers were far less puffy and the skin on his palm was no longer an angry red.

As she went to put the item away, a thought occurred to her. She could do something else for her male, even though he might be angry at her if she did it. Still, she was tempted. She'd thought it would take hours of tissue massage and ointments to break down the scars on his back, but the dermal regen could do it much faster.

Still, she hesitated. She wanted to ease the pain that shadowed him night and day, but if she did it without his consent, she'd only be causing him a different kind of pain.

No, she decided. She couldn't make that choice for him. Once he was fully healed, she'd talk to him about it again. She could try to make him see that he didn't need to suffer anymore. It would be easy enough to leave the scars as a visible reminder while correcting the twisted snarls of scar tissue that caused him pain.

She finished packing up the med-kit and set it aside before curling up behind Menace, her arm draped over his chest so she could feel his every breath.

She'd spent so much of her life without many choices. She wouldn't take this one from him.

## 11

WHEN MENACE FIRST WOKE UP, he couldn't remember where he was or how he'd gotten there. Once he dredged up a few scattered memories, he went from wondering where he was, to trying to figure out how he was still alive. Shatter had died after being stung by one of the creatures. Why hadn't he?

He raised his injured hand in front of his face and examined it in the light of a glow-pod Hope must have set out before she'd gone to sleep. Apart from a little swelling, his hand looked fine. He carefully closed his fingers into a fist and only felt a minor twinge of discomfort. Not surprising given the amount of toxin the nameless blue squishy thing had pumped into his hand as it died.

Hope had saved him. Gratitude for what she'd done mixed with wonder that his little beauty had the skills and determination to heal him. Not only that, she'd *defied* him. He remembered that. He'd told her to leave him and get back to the cave, and she'd *growled* at him, given him orders, and then treated him with a gentle, caring manner he'd never experienced with anyone else.

He rolled over so he could look at her. Her dark hair with its streaks of white reminded him of moonlight dancing on the river at night, and he wondered how someone as gentle and lovely as this female could belong to him. She could have left him to die on the shore and no one would have known what happened. She could have sought out Bysshe or one of the others to protect her, but she'd stayed with him. She'd fought to keep him alive. She'd chosen *him*.

*"I'm yours. Remember?"* Her words from yesterday came back to him.

"Mine," he said.

Hope stirred and then yawned before opening her eyes. "Are you feeling better?"

"Much. Thanks to you."

Her eyes shimmered with water again, and he a vague recollection that some species did that when they felt strong emotions. *Tears?* Was that the word?

She sat up and threw her arms around him. "Good. I was so worried at first. I thought I might lose you."

The tears spilled down her cheeks and wet his fur where she had her face pressed against him.

"I am here, little beauty. You stayed with me when I needed you. Thank you for that."

She made a snuffling noise and squeezed him tighter. "Of course I stayed. You needed me." She drew in a soft breath before adding, "And I need you."

"But not for protection. You proved that yesterday. So why, little beauty?"

She gave him a look that reminded him of Bysshe when he thought one of his brothers had said something too stupid to be believed. "Why? Because of this," she laid a hand on his chest, right where the strange new marks intersected. "And because you think I'm beautiful and worth protecting. And well, dammit, because I'm pretty sure I'm falling in love with you."

"You are worth protecting. And beautiful, and smart, and..." he trailed off. "You love me?"

"Can we forget I said that aloud? I mean, we met a hot second ago, and this could all be hormones, or pheromones, or straight-up lust. I mean, I am the first female you've ever seen. Right? It's only you and your brothers here, and the verexi are genderless and asexual."

"No," he growled and hauled her up against him. "I will not forget you said that. No one has ever said anything like that to me before. Feelings..." He shook his head. "I don't do those very well. None of us do. But I want you to stay with me. I need you, Hope. I may love you too, but I don't know what that feels like. I just know that when I thought I was dying, leaving you behind was the only regret I had. I didn't want to lose you."

She kissed him. "That's love, or the start of it."

"Then it's settled." He rolled onto his back so she was straddling him again. "You love me. I love you. We don't need to speak of this again."

Hope laughed, a sound so bright and joyful it made him want to join in. "That's not how it works, Ace. It's like a plant…"

He grimaced, and she laughed again. "Okay, it's like an animal. You have to feed and care for it if you want it to grow. Love needs to be nurtured."

He huffed. "That still sounds like a plant to me."

"There's nothing wrong with plants. You carve wood. Don't you? That comes from plants."

He drew her head down to kiss her, letting his tongue slide into her mouth for a long, slow kiss before answering. "I carve the corpses of plants into pleasing shapes. That's not the same thing as liking them."

"You are the most difficult, stubborn male—

He pulled back and touched his finger to her lips to quiet her. She immediately fell silent.

He lifted her off of him and set her down on the mattress before gesturing for her to get under the covers and stay there. Someone was coming.

He didn't speak, but he made sure his hand signals were clear. Hope nodded once and then did her best to melt into the shadows at the far end of the sleeping area while covering herself with the hides strewn over the bed.

He didn't wait for her to finish. Whoever was out there, he needed to deal with them. He stopped at the wall with the wide array of weapons, selecting a long, vicious blade he'd forged a few months ago. It was one of his better attempts, though he didn't often get a chance to use it. He waited for the blood lust to rise up the way it always did when he was about to go on the hunt, but nothing happened.

Strange.

He glanced back at Hope for a moment, pleased to see she'd hidden herself well. He would not let anything happen to her. No mercenary would ever lay hands on his little beauty. He'd kill anyone who tried.

It was possible the distant voices belonged to some of his clanmates, though they rarely traveled together for long, and it was rare for them to enter another brother's territory without announcing themselves.

The voices faded before they got close enough for him to identify, leaving him straining to hear any sign of approach.

It didn't take long before he heard a twig snap nearby. The enemy was here.

He roared, flung the door aside, and then charged out into the morning sun, one hand shielding his eyes as he looked for someone to fight.

"Shit!" a familiar voice yelled.

"Menace, easy. Dammit, I told you two that sneaking up on him was a stupid idea."

He finally caught sight of a familiar face. "Havoc?"

"It's me. Well, us. I'm with Vengeance and Risk. It was their idea to try and sneak up the last bit to see if you heard us."

"I heard you," he snarled and lowered his weapon, but he didn't let go of it. "I heard you speaking when you were still halfway down the fucking mountain. Why are you here?"

Havoc knew about this place because he'd helped Menace transport the supplies now stashed in the cave. Menace had done the same for him.

Risk answered his question. "We're on our way to join the others to search for survivors from the crash. The big ship that came down two days ago. You know about that. Right? You were with Mayhem and Strife when it happened?"

"I know, but not about anything else. Tell me more." he said.

Vengeance spoke next. "The rest of our brothers are already on their way to the area where we think the ship went down. Bysshe sent word yesterday morning, but the three of us were out hunting and only got back last night. We're taking a shortcut to catch up."

Havoc nodded. "If we're last to arrive, there may not be any females left for us."

They knew about the females, but if they thought they could simply arrive and claim one, they were in for a surprise. Menace decided not to warn them. They could figure it out for themselves. The idiots should never have tried to sneak up on him.

"Mayhem found one. A female. Did you know that? Bysshe said he has markings now, and so does she..." Risk cut himself off and pointed to Menace. "What the fuck is on your chest?"

Before he could answer, Vengeance snarled and bared his fangs. "You bastard. You found one of them. Didn't you?"

Menace didn't answer.

"Can we see her?" Havoc asked.

"No! She's mine!" he snarled and took a step toward Havoc, who snarled back but didn't otherwise move.

He raised the blade and shook his head in warning. "You need to leave. *Now.*"

None of them reacted. Instead, all three of them stared past him in wide-eyed astonishment.

He knew what they were staring at even before he turned his head. Hope stood in the cave entrance. Her hair was still mussed from sleeping and all she wore was the cut-down robe she'd had on when they met. Now that other males were present, he regretted cutting away so much.

"Menace, are these your brothers?" she asked in a soft voice that seemed to melt the edge off his anger.

"Yes. Now go back inside," he demanded as he pointed to the entrance.

"She's beautiful," Havoc said quietly.

"That's what Menace says, too." Hope ignored his instructions and his warning growl. She walked up beside him, set her hand on his back, and stroked his fur gently.

"Hope…" He turned her name into another growl, but all she did was lean into his side and smile.

"Stop it, Ace. They're not going to do anything to me." She stood a little straighter and raised her arms so that her markings were on display. "They can see that I belong to you."

The moment she said those words, his anger faded, and he lowered the blade while wrapping a possessive arm around her. "Mine," he confirmed.

"Right. Yours. I can see that," Havoc said and all three of them stepped back a little.

That was better.

"See? They understand. And if they're lucky, maybe some of the survivors will want to be theirs." She smiled at his brothers and a note of iron filled her voice. "If you find anyone alive, match or not, be good to them. They've been through a lot." She looked up at him and beamed. "Be gentle, like my mate was with me."

He waited for one of them to laugh or make a joke about him ever being gentle, but none of them did. They all nodded and stared at Hope like she was the only star in the damned sky.

After a few more seconds, he'd had enough. If they

wanted to look at a female, they could find their own. "If you don't hurry, you'll be the last to arrive. Better run." He pointed toward the river. "There's a shallow crossing about a mile upstream. If you see any supplies, leave them. They belong to me." He gave them a bemused smile. "And watch out for the blue stinging things. One got me yesterday."

Risk looked confused. "If you'd been stung by one, why are you still alive?"

His chest swelled with pride as he answered his brother. "Because my mate is not only beautiful, she is trained in medicine. The clan will be better off now that she is with us. With *me*." He deliberately turned and kissed her on the lips, ignoring his three brothers' stares. "Hope is mine." He pointed to the river again. "Go find your own."

He moved Hope behind him and then allowed the others to approach for their ritual goodbye. All of them butted heads, their horns clacking as they connected. "Good hunting," he said.

Havoc grinned, his gaze flicking to Hope for a brief moment. "Enjoy the spoils of your hunt, brother."

"That I will."

They left seconds later, leaving him and Hope alone on the hill.

"They seem nice," Hope said.

"They are *not* nice. They are stubborn, arrogant asses. All of them. And you should have stayed inside!" He tried to tower over her, but she reached up and put both hands on his horns, dragging him down to her level.

"Hush. No one is around to be impressed by your bluster. I know your secret. Remember?"

He bared his fangs and growled, "For the last time, female. I am *not* sweet!"

She laughed and kissed him. "Maybe not. But I love you anyway."

Those words flowed over him like cool water, washing away the last of his anger. He didn't understand how or why she affected him that way, but he was grateful for it.

He dropped his weapon, swept her into his arms, and carried her toward the entrance.

"Where are we going?" she asked, though she had to know the answer already.

"My brothers' arrival interrupted my plans. Now they have gone..."

"Does this plan include bed rest? As your doctor, I'd advise you to get plenty of it."

"Bed, yes. Rest?" He chuckled and kissed her as he stepped inside. "Rest is not part of my plan."

He set her down on the floor close to his bed and then took a step back. Now they were alone, he wanted her naked again. "Undress."

She laughed and undid the knot in the belt before slipping out of the tattered robe and letting it fall to the floor.

He nodded and pointed to the bed. "You. There. Now."

"What happened to your vocabulary?" she asked.

He pointed to his rock-hard cock. "All the blood has left my brain."

She went to stretch out on the bed and he took a moment to scoop up the robe she'd worn. Without a word he balled it up and tossed it out the door.

"Hey! That's my only clothing!"

"We have a fabricator. Bysshe will make you new clothes. Pretty ones that will cover more of your body when we are around my clanmates."

He prowled over to her, dropping to his knees once he reached the mattress, and crawled the last bit of distance. He could smell her need already, a sweet, musky scent that he'd crave for the rest of his life. He moved over her, one knee between her thighs so her pussy was exposed and her body laid out like a feast beneath him.

"Who do you belong to?" he asked as he cupped her sex in his hand. He moved slowly, teasing her as he gently slid his middle finger into her wet, heated folds.

Hope moaned and writhed on the mattress, her eyes almost closed. "You. I'm yours, Menace."

He stroked the callused pad of his finger over her clit, and she shivered in response. "Never forget that. You are mine. I will protect you and pleasure you for the rest of your life." He added another finger and sped up his movements. He needed to prepare her and his control was already slipping. He took his cock in his free hand and pumped the shaft, trying to buy himself a few more seconds.

"I won't forget." Her eyes opened and the look she gave him held more than need. It was full of trust, acceptance, and other emotions he couldn't name, because he'd never seen them before. Never *felt* them.

She arched her hips and opened her arms to him. "I love you, and I *need* you. Now, Menace. Fuck me."

That was one order he was happy to obey.

He settled over her, his cock pressed to the seam of her pussy and hands planted beside her shoulders. His mouth was only a breath away from hers. "As my little beauty wishes." He leaned in and kissed her, heat flaring between them as his mouth ravished hers.

She twined one leg around his hips and arched upward, bringing their bodies together as their tongues dueled. It only took a second and a twist of his hips to align himself with her entrance, and then he was inside her, sliding into her silken heat.

She was his haven, and the pleasure he felt right now was better than anything he'd ever imagined while he'd suffered through years of cruelty and abuse. When he was with her, the past lost its grip on him, and he could see a future filled with more than just vengeance and death.

Her tiny fingernails raked across his shoulders and she moaned into his mouth as he pounded into her, every hard thrust and bruising kiss carrying them closer to the edge.

Her inner walls fluttered around his cock, telling him she was on the brink. He didn't slow down, not even when she gasped his name, shuddering as her orgasm hit.

He kept going, letting her pleasure magnify his until his own release hit with all the force of a meteor strike. He emptied himself inside her, his entire body shuddering as he thrust one last time before his ridges swelled, locking them together.

That sent another shiver through Hope, her soft gasps exploding against his lips and cheeks as she dusted his face with kisses.

"It's official," she whispered a moment later.

"Mhm? What's that?" he asked.

"I definitely love you, Ace. No one else had ever made me feel the way you do."

He chuckled and nuzzled her cheek. "Satisfied?"

"Well, yeah. That too. But that's not what I meant. Being with you feels right. Like I've finally found my place in this cold, unforgiving universe."

He raised his head just enough that he could look into her beautiful eyes. "I know where my place is, too. By your side. Now and always."

He kissed her again, gently this time.

Today was the best day of his life. He'd gone looking for the enemy... and found his future.

Hope.

# EPILOGUE

"Do you think they'll be here soon?" Hope asked for what she knew had to be the twentieth time in the last hour. Restlessness made it impossible for her to sit still, so she'd taken to wandering around her new home and checking on things she'd already checked a dozen times.

"Soon," Menace said. Unlike her, he wasn't concerned about their impending guests. He lounged in a massive chair, a metal mug of cool water in his hand. "Why are you so concerned? You know these females."

"I do. I mean, I know them a little. We were all rejects, and most of us kept to ourselves. Rissa helped me to the escape pods. I know her a little. But I barely spoke to Bella. She always seemed so, uh, together. I found her a little intimidating."

Her mate scowled. "Did she do something to you?

Say something? She will not be welcome inside our home if she did."

"No! Nothing like that. I just respected her too much to bother her. Does that make sense?"

"No," Menace stated. "But a lot of human behaviors make no sense to me."

She stopped her aimless wandering to glare at him. "You only know one human, and I've only been here a few days. I am not that hard to understand."

"If you say so."

She huffed in mock frustration and went over to check on the refreshments she'd prepared for today. Fruits and even some nuts Bysshe had assured her were safe for human consumption along with water and fruit juices she'd squeezed herself. The males would eat meat, of course. She'd put out some of the cured and dried meats Menace kept in a pantry off the main house.

The main house. The thought made her smile. Menace's home was nothing like she'd expected. Instead of a bigger cave or a simple shack, he resided in a treehouse—a large one with a massive, railed deck, the three-room house, and several other small structures, including the pantry and a shed that housed his precious store of batteries.

The batteries were recharged by several wind turbines set up nearby. Apparently, some of the others had small hydro-electric systems, too. They had power, simple appliances, and even running water of a sort.

They'd engineered a system of cisterns and gravity-fed pipes to supply all their homes with a rudimentary toilet, shower, and water for drinking. It was a simple life, but it had far more comforts than she'd expected, and strangely enough, it reminded her of her childhood home.

She lifted her head to ask again when they'd be arriving, but Menace held up a hand and laughed. "Soon, little beauty. The others had to go back to their homes and collect their mates to bring them here."

"Right. And you live farther back on your land than the others." He'd explained that to her, but she'd forgotten.

Menace had met up with Mayhem and Strife yesterday and again this morning. Like her mate, they'd found survivors in the other escape pods, and they'd worked together to bring every bit of gear back to their community. Most of it went to Bysshe, but some, especially the meal packs, were split up for the women to use.

She'd met Bysshe that morning. Menace had introduced the android and left them to talk while he went with the others. She'd told Bysshe everything she could remember about Rage and the news stories about the verexi and the fa'rel. He'd asked questions that had helped her remember even more information, and she'd felt like she could trust him.

It was a nice feeling.

Menace clearly didn't trust any of his brothers as

much as he did Bysshe, though. Because she had yet to reunite with Bella and Rissa, Bysshe had explained it wasn't just her mate. All three of the males had become overprotective and possessive of their women as soon as they'd gained their mating marks. That's what they'd decided to call them.

In the end, it had taken all three women to enlist Bysshe to their cause as he'd visited each of them. Eventually he made the males agree to have a get-together.

Bysshe had smiled as he confessed to her that morning. "You may have noticed that your mate is quite aggressive. The other two are concerned about what might happen if they inadvertently piss him off while you're around."

She'd laughed. "Tell them if that happens I'll deal with him. He's better with me."

"I will do that." His blue-black eyes had crinkled at the corners at that. "And I'm glad to hear it. They—*we*—all have scars, but Menace carries more than most.

"I know. But now they know that Rage is still out there, alive and well. I think that helps."

"It does," the android had agreed.

Thoughts of her meeting with the blue-skinned android had distracted her so well she almost didn't hear Menace say her name.

"Hope?"

"Mm? What?"

"They're here."

She flew out of the house and onto the deck. There they were! She waved and laughed as she spotted the other two human women and their large, furry mates.

"You made it!" Rissa called up to her, waving back.

"So did you! I'm so glad!" she called back. She'd expected to be happy to see them, but she felt so much more than that: relief, joy, happiness, and other things too complex to address right now, like the guilt of seeing these two and wondering if anyone else was still alive.

Tears wet her cheeks as she flew down the stairs that wound down the trunk of the massive tree that was now her home.

Rissa reached her first, and the two embraced as if they were long-lost friends instead of recent acquaintances. Bella joined in, and the three of them hugged, cried, and laughed while all three of their mates looked on with bewildered expressions.

Finally, Menace spoke up. "I don't understand this human behavior, either."

"The water from their eyes is called tears. They indicate sadness," Strife said. At least she thought it was Strife since he'd been the one with Rissa.

"Sadness? I thought they wanted to see each other," the other one said. "Falling star, why are you sad?"

Bella laughed and smiled at her mate. "Tears are sometimes happy things, too."

Mayhem grumbled. "This is why I have such

trouble understanding my painted beauty. Humans are confusing."

"We are not!" All three of them said at once, which led to another round of hugs and laughter.

Eventually they all made their way up the stairs to her new home, and spent the next few hours eating, drinking, and comparing stories.

It was the best day of her life, she decided, and then immediately changed her mind. No, it was the *second* best.

The most wonderful day of all was when she'd crashed onto a prison planet and discovered a life she'd never planned for and a love beyond her wildest dreams.

∼

***

**Thank You for Reading Marked For Menace.**

Want to read Hope and Menace's special bonus epilogue? Sign up for my newsletter here: subscribepage.io/Bonuscontent

And if you want to know how Risk, Vengeance, and Havoc are fairing, next up is Marked For Risk.

Want to read more stories with book boyfriends
that are out of this world?

Check out Susan Hayes' other Science Fiction
Romance Series at
**_Susanhayes.ca_**

# ABOUT THE AUTHOR

Susan lives out on the Canadian west coast surrounded by open water, dear family, and good friends. She's jumped out of perfectly good airplanes on purpose and accidentally swum with sharks on the Great Barrier Reef.

If the world ends, she plans to survive as the spunky, comedic sidekick to the heroes of the new world, because she's too damned short and out of shape to make it on her own for long.

*You can find out more about Susan and her books at:*
www.susanhayes.ca